"OUT OF THE FRYING PAN..."

Our Story So Far...

Dr. Ping, the "Blue Tiger" that has secretly spread anarchy within the Japanese troops, succeeds in smuggling Terry and Hu-Shee out of a Jap camp. On their way, it is becoming increasingly obvious that Terry and Hu-Shee are warming up to each other, but a dashing pilot former friend of Hu-Shee crash-lands near them and comes into the scene like a hair in the soup...

ISBN 0-918348-76-5
LC 87-090446

© NBM 1989
cover designed and painted by Ray Fehrenbach.

Terry & The Pirates is a registered trademark of the Tribune Media Services, Inc.

THE FLYING BUTTRESS CLASSICS LIBRARY
is an imprint of:

NANTIER·BEALL·MINOUSTCHINE
Publishing co.
new york

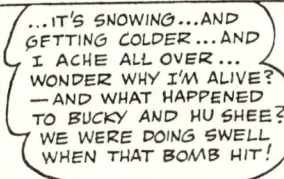

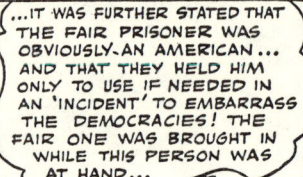

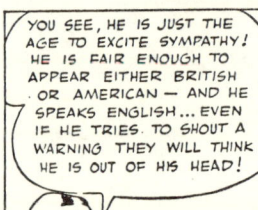

JOLLY GOOD, NUMBER THREE! NOW, IF YOU GENTLEMEN WILL JUST LOOK AFTER THOSE ARCHIES FORE AND AFT, I WILL ATTEMPT TO FIND A HOME FOR THIS CIGAR I'M CARRYING!
4-20
YOU HAVE DONE THIS TO DISCREDIT ME WITH THE HIGH COMMAND! MY RAFT WILL BE CALLED A FAILUIRE! I WILL REPORT YOU FOR HIGH TREASON!
YOU WILL HAVE A LONG SWIM! ...OFF OF MY BRIDGE, YOU - - YOU LANDSMAN!
4-21
Reg. U. S. Pat. Off.; Copyright, 1941, by News Syndicate Co. Inc.
THE PLANES HAVE CLIMBED OUT OF RANGE, MY CAPTAIN! WE ARE SINKING RAPIDLY, SIR!
ABANDON THE SHIP!
I HAVE FAILED! I WILL BE KEPT OUT OF MY RIGHTFUL PLACE IN THE GOVERNMENT AGAIN! ..... AND YOU ARE THE CAUSE OF IT!
MILTON CANIFF
YOU ORDERED THE BATTERIES TO FIRE ON THE BRITISH PLANES, TO EXPOSE US AS A RAIDER! YOU CAUSED THE FAILURE OF KIEL'S RAFT!
DO YOU THINK THEY'D OBEY SOMEONE GIVING ORDERS IN ENGLISH? BESIDES, I WAS IN THE BRIG!
4-22
Reg. U. S. Pat. Off.; Copyright, 1941, by News Syndicate Co. Inc.
THEN WHY AREN'T YOU STILL IN THE BRIG — SO YOU COULD DROWN LIKE THE RAT YOU ARE?
BECAUSE THE CAPTAIN ORDERED ALL PRISONERS RELEASED WHEN THE SHIP WENT INTO ACTION! SOME PEOPLE ARE STILL CIVILIZED!
THEN KIEL WILL REMEDY THAT! IT WILL BE SOME SATISFACTION TO KNOW YOU WENT DOWN WITH THE SHIP! THINK OF THE HONOR — YOU WILL BE LOCKED IN THE CAPTAIN'S CABIN!
MILTON CANIFF

READY TO LOWER AWAY THE LAST BOAT, MY CAPTAIN!
VERY WELL! I WILL GET THE CODE BOOKS AND LOG FROM MY CABIN!
4-23
Reg. U. S. Pat. Off. Copyright, 1941, by News Syndicate Co. Inc.
KIEL! WHY ARE YOU AND THE BOY NOT IN A LIFE-BOAT? I ORDERED THE SHIP ABANDONED!
I WILL BE IN A MOMENT!
THIS FOOL IS THE CAUSE OF OUR TROUBLES! I AM LEAVING HIM TO DROWN!
MILTON CANIFF
RELEASE THAT BOY AND GO TO YOUR PLACE IN THE BOAT! YOU MAY BE A PET OF THE HIGH COMMAND— BUT I AM CAPTAIN OF THIS SHIP!

4-24
Reg. U. S. Pat. Off. Copyright, 1941, by News Syndicate Co. Inc.
OH--- I'M FINISHED! GO TO THE---BOAT --YOU TWO---
KIEL WILL GO TO THE BOAT! THE YOUNG FOOL CAN BE LOCKED IN TO HOLD YOUR HAND!
MILTON CANIFF

4-25
Reg. U. S. Pat. Off. Copyright, 1941, by News Syndicate Co. Inc.
TOO MANY CLOTHES... ...SUCTION PULLING ME DOWN...
MILTON CANIFF

THAT WAS A FOOL THING TO DO... WE MIGHT HAVE BEEN SUCKED DOWN BY THE SHIP, TRYING TO SAVE THE AMERICAN!
BUT WE WEREN'T! ... AND A SURVIVOR IS A SURVIVOR, NO MATTER WHAT HIS NATIONALITY! WARM THE YOUNG ONE UP A BIT!
4-26
Reg. U. S. Pat. Off. Copyright, 1941, by News Syndicate Co. Inc.
...THE BOY'S A BAD PENNY! WE COME HALF WAY AROUND THE WORLD TO RAID SHIPPING... GET ONE VICTIM... THEN GET SUNK!
NOT OUR FAULT! I HEAR A SPY ON BOARD GAVE THE FIRST ORDER TO FIRE ON THE PLANES!
PROBABLY THIS AMERICAN!
...NO! HE WAS IN THE SHIP'S PRISON WHEN IT HAPPENED! ...IT WAS A MEMBER OF THE CREW! SOME BRITISHER WHO GOT INTO OUR NAVY!... THE SECRET POLICE WILL CATCH HIM!
MILTON CANIFF
HUH! I WOULD LIKE TO GET MY HAND ON HIM THIS MINUTE!

Reg. U. S. Pat. Off.; Copyright, 1941, by News Syndicate Co. Inc.
TERRY AND THE PIRATES
by MILTON CANIFF
THE HIGH COMMAND ORDERS THAT YOU SURVIVORS OF THE TORPEDOED RAIDER ARE TO REMAIN HERE UNTIL ANOTHER SHIP IS READY!...
IT WOULD NOT BE WELL FOR THE BRITISH TO KNOW THAT WE ARE BASING OUR PACIFIC RAIDERS AT THIS PORT — SO DO NOT ADVERTISE YOUR PRESENCE!
...WHO IS THE BLONDE ONE UPSTAIRS ?
AN AMERICAN, EXCELLENCY! HE WAS BROUGHT BY KIEL TO SERVE AS DECOY ON THE TORPEDO RAFT! WE CARRIED HIM ASHORE AFTER THE PLANES SANK OUR SHIP!...
27
...THERE ARE NO FACILITIES FOR DEALING WITH SUPERCARGO! BE RID OF HIM!
...BUT HOW, EXCELLENCY?
MUST I GIVE YOU AN ILLUSTRATED GUIDE?—THE OCEAN IS DEEP!
MY REPORT SAYS THERE WAS A FRIEND OF KIEL'S— A MADAME LUSTRE! SHE MAY HAVE INFORMATION OF HIS THAT COULD BE SOLD TO THE ENEMY! SHE IS TO BE ELIMINATED! DO YOU KNOW OF HER?
NO, EXCELLENCY! WE SAW KIEL ONLY WHEN HE CAME ABOARD OUR SHIP!
NO MATTER! SHE IS DOUBTLESS IN THE CITY! OUR AGENTS WILL FIND HER VERY QUICKLY!
...HEARD HIM MENTION BURMA'S ASSUMED NAME!... WISH I UNDERSTOOD THEIR LANGUAGE BETTER!.. MAYBE THEY'RE AFTER HER!
OOP YOU GO, YOONG FELLER!
OH, YOU SPEAK ENGLISH?...WHAT ARE THEY GOING TO DO WITH ME?
VELL... I DON'DT LIKE TO TELL YOO... BUT DOT SEE-GRIT POLICER SAID YOO VUZ TO BE POOT OUDT OF ZIRCULATION!
GONNA KILL ME? —BUT THEY DIDN'T LEARN ABOUT THE SIGNAL FLAGS!... OH, GOLLY!..
BUT WHY?
DOT SEE-GRIT POLICER SAYS YOU ARE A NOOZANCE! VE GODT NO CHOIZE! ORDERS ISS ORDERS!
BUT LISTEN—THERE'S A GIRL... I CAN'T DIE LIKE THIS... NO! LISTEN...
NO! NO!
IT VILL BE QUIGLY OAFER!... I SEE IF DOZE ROPES ARE GOOT UND TIGHDT!
I'M CUTTING THE ROPE, OLD BOY!— HOLD THE ROCK AND SINK OUT OF SIGHT! THERE'S AN ADDRESS ON THIS PAPER... THE PEOPLE THERE WILL HELP YOU! TELL THEM AGENT R-61 SAID TO KEEP THUMBS UP! ...CHEER'O!
THROWING HELPLESS BOYS INTO THE SEA IS NOT MY IDEA OF WAR...THIS IS A BAD BUSINESS!
...HUSH! CRITICISM OF ORDERS MAY BRING A WORSE FATE UPON YOU!... HE IS PROBABLY IN A HAPPIER PLACE BY NOW!

THE LAST SPOT IN THE WORLD I EVER EXPECTED TO FIND A BRITISH SPY — ON A RAIDER!.... HE MUST HAVE BEEN THE GUY WHO SHOT THE GUN THAT TIPPED OFF THE PLANES!
4-28
Reg. U. S. Pat. Off.: Copyright, 1941, by News Syndicate Co. Inc.
THE CHANCES PEOPLE TAKE IN WARTIME!... WITH KIEL GONE THEY DON'T WANT TO BE BOTHERED WITH ME.... BUT THEY'LL BEAR DOWN ON BURMA, BECAUSE SHE KNOWS TOO MUCH! THAT SPY GAVE ME THE ADDRESS OF A PLACE WHERE I MIGHT GET HELP!
THE PAPER LOOKS LIKE PART OF AN ADVERTISEMENT! I MAY GET A KNIFE IN ME — BUT I HAVE TO TAKE THE CHANCE!.... HERE'S THE HOUSE! GUESS I'D BETTER KNOCK!...
NO ANSWER! GUESS THEY DIDN'T HEAR ME!
MILTON CANIFF

OH!
WHO WANTS WHO?
4-29
Reg. U. S. Pat. Off.: Copyright, 1941, by News Syndicate Co. Inc.
MY NAME IS TERRY LEE! I WAS TOLD TO BRING THIS PAPER HERE... BY A MAN WHO CALLED HIMSELF R-61!
NEVER HEARD OF SAME! ...CALL MASTER!
MASTER, A VERY DAMP YOUNG ONE COMES WITH PAPER!... HE SAY SENT BY R-61!
SO! WE SHALL SEE IF HE LIES!
MILTON CANIFF
YUN SAN
O. YIN
IMPORTER
14 Lilya Rd.
Identification for R-61

R-61 IS CLEVER! HE DOES NOT RISK HIS PLACE ON THE RAIDER CREW BY COMING HERE!... INSTEAD HE SENDS A YOUNG ONE WITH PROPER CREDENTIALS! BRING THE BOY TO ME!
4-30
Reg. U. S. Pat. Off.: Copyright, 1941, by News Syndicate Co. Inc.
...YOUR CLOTHES WILL BE DRIED AND SEARCHED! YOU MAY BATHE WHILE YOU TELL ME YOUR STORY, MR. TERRY LEE!
THAT'S A GOOD STUNT TO KEEP ME FROM RUNNING AWAY... BUT IT'S PLENTY OKAY BY ME!
MEANWHILE...
NO WORD FROM TERRY OR KIEL!... WHAT IF THEY FOUND THOSE SIGNAL FLAGS ON THE KID AND TOSSED HIM TO THE TUNA!... I FEEL SORTA UNEASY!
THE WOMAN KNOWN AS MADAME LUSTRE LIVES IN THIS BUILDING! SHE PROBABLY DOESN'T KNOW OF KIEL'S DEATH — SO IT IS ROUTINE SECRET POLICE BUSINESS TO ELIMINATE HER BEFORE SHE TALKS TOO MUCH! I WILL ATTEND TO IT PERSONALLY... MIGHT BE AN AMUSING DIVERSION!
MILTON CANIFF

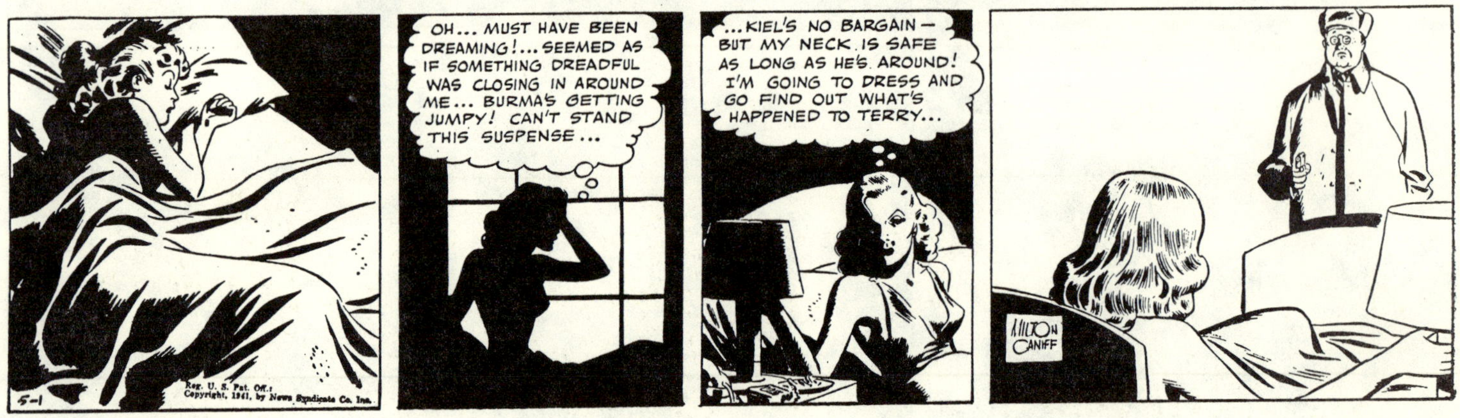
5-1
Reg. U. S. Pat. Off.: Copyright, 1941, by News Syndicate Co. Inc.
OH... MUST HAVE BEEN DREAMING!... SEEMED AS IF SOMETHING DREADFUL WAS CLOSING IN AROUND ME... BURMA'S GETTING JUMPY! CAN'T STAND THIS SUSPENSE...
...KIEL'S NO BARGAIN — BUT MY NECK IS SAFE AS LONG AS HE'S AROUND! I'M GOING TO DRESS AND GO FIND OUT WHAT'S HAPPENED TO TERRY...
MILTON CANIFF

YOU NEED NOT REACH FOR THE TELEPHONE, MADAME LUSTRE!... YOU SEE, I AM HERE THROUGH THE CO-OPERATION OF THE MANAGEMENT!
THAT MAKES IT NICE! I SUPPOSE YOU ARE MAKING A SURVEY TO SEE HOW THE GUESTS LIKE THE VIEW AT DAWN!
HMM... THE LADY IS NOT ONLY QUITE A BEAUTY — BUT SHE MAKES LITTLE JOKES IN THE PRESENCE OF DANGER!
OH, SURE... THEY CALL ME THE GIGGLING GODIVA! WHAT CAN I DO FOR YOU, POP?
I CAME HERE TO PUT YOU OUT OF THE WAY... SINCE YOUR FRIEND KIEL DIED WHEN THE RAIDER SANK...
THE RAIDER SANK?... WH-WHAT ABOUT THE MEN?
A FEW OF THE REGULAR CREW MEMBERS WERE SAVED... THAT IS ALL!
NOT CONCERNED ABOUT HER OWN FUTURE... PERHAPS SHE REALLY CARED FOR THIS KIEL! THOSE TEARS ARE GENUINE!
MILTON CANIFF
5-2
Reg. U. S. Pat. Off.: Copyright, 1941, by News Syndicate Co. Inc.

I HARDLY EXPECTED SUCH A DISPLAY OF EMOTION OVER THIS MAN KIEL GOING DOWN WITH THE RAIDER AND MOST OF HER CREW!
...DON'T BE SURPRISED AT ANYTHING I DO!.... WELL, POP, I DON'T SUPPOSE YOU'D RECONSIDER WHAT YOU SAID ABOUT CASHING IN MY CHIPS!
YOU KNOW TOO MUCH ABOUT KIEL'S BUSINESS IN THE ORIENT! IT IS THE HIGH COMMAND'S POLICY TO KEEP OUR ACTIVITIES HERE QUIET — FOR THE MOMENT!
AFRAID I'LL SELL OUT, HUH?
ON THE OTHER HAND — YOU MIGHT BE VERY VALUABLE TO OUR SECRET POLICE — UNDER PROPER SUPERVISION, OF COURSE!... SUPPOSE YOU DRESS WHILE I CONSIDER THE MATTER FURTHER!
KIEL'S DEAD... TERRY'S DEAD! LOOK AT YOURSELF, FACE... YOU'RE STILL IN ONE PIECE BY A NARROW MARGIN! YOU GET BURMA INTO TROUBLE, AND YOU GET HER OUT! MIGHT AS WELL PUT ON A NEW COAT OF PAINT AND START ANOTHER CAMPAIGN TO KEEP OUT OF THE BREADLINE!
MILTON CANIFF
5-3
Reg. U. S. Pat. Off.: Copyright, 1941, by News Syndicate Co. Inc.

TERRY AND THE PIRATES
by MILTON CANIFF
....WE ARE SATISFIED AS TO YOUR IDENTITY, MR. TERRY LEE!
BUT THAT'S NOT THE ONLY IMPORTANT THING! I TELL YOU THE SECRET POLICE OF KIEL'S COUNTRY ARE GOING TO ELIMINATE THIS MADAME LUSTRE — BECAUSE SHE PROBABLY KNOWS TOO MUCH!
... THAT IS UNDERSTANDABLE! NO DOUBT THEY HAVE ALREADY FOUND THE WOMAN!
... BUT YOU WORK FOR THE BRITISH!... IF YOU HELP HER OUT OF THIS MESS SHE WOULD TELL YOU WHAT SHE KNOWS! SHE DOESN'T GIVE A HOOT WHO WINS THE WAR!
ONE NEVER KNOWS! — BUT THERE IS LOGIC IN YOUR PLEA!... COME, LET US DISTURB OURSELVES INTO ACTION!...
... AS A ROUTINE MATTER WE KNOW WHERE THIS MADAME LUSTRE LIVES! THE SECRET POLICE OF KIEL'S PEOPLE, PLUS THE INVADER MILITARY GUARD, ARE NO DOUBT IN FULL POSSESSION OF THE PREMISES AT THIS MOMENT! OUR FIRST MOVE IS TO INFORM YOUR LADY FRIEND THAT YOU ARE ACTIVE ON HER BEHALF!...
MEANWHILE...
... LET US BE FRANK, WOMAN!... YOU KNOW I AM OF THE SECRET POLICE! I KNOW YOU ARE MORE OF AN OPPORTUNIST THAN A SPY FOR MY COUNTRY'S ENEMIES!
AND NOW THAT WE'VE UNMASKED, YOU WANT THE NEXT WALTZ!

YOU AMERICANS ARE SO DROLL!... I THINK WE UNDERSTAND EACH OTHER! ... I CAME HERE TO PUT YOU OUT OF THE WAY BECAUSE YOU KNOW TOO MUCH! I DID NOT EXPECT TO FIND SUCH A BEAUTY!
...AND SINCE KIEL IS GONE YOU WANT ME TO WEAR YOUR FRATERNITY PIN!
...YOU CAN BE VERY VALUABLE TO ME IF YOU CHOOSE... AND YOU WILL BE WELL PAID!...I NEED NOT REMIND YOU THAT IF YOU REFUSE IT WILL BE MY UNPLEASANT DUTY TO CARRY OUT MY ORIGINAL PURPOSE IN COMING HERE!
NOTHING LIKE HAVING A WIDE RANGE OF EVILS TO SELECT FROM!
WELL, THE MERRY-GO-ROUND IS BUSTED AGAIN! THE ROYAL AIR FORCE PUNCHED OUT BURMA'S MEAL TICKET!....AND TERRY'S GONE, TOO! HE WAS A GOOD KID...SORTA REMINDED ME OF NICE CLEAN THINGS I HAD FORGOTTEN EXISTED! ...NOW THIS PUFFY PUNK WANTS ME TO JOIN HIS MATA HARI TEAM! —AND I'M TOO TIRED TO RESIST!
...IF THE KID HADN'T CHECKED OUT I MIGHT PUT UP A FIGHT... WE COULD HAVE SHAKEN LOOSE SOMEHOW!... BUT WHAT'S THE USE TO---
SOME ONE KNOCKING! DO NOT MOVE! I WILL ANSWER IT!
EXCELLENCY! A CHINESE BOY BROUGHT THIS PACKAGE FOR MADAME LUSTRE! I INSPECTED IT FOR CONCEALED WEAPONS OR A MESSAGE ... BUT IT IS A PLAIN BOLT OF MATERIAL!
DO YOU KNOW WHAT THIS IS, MADAME?
5-4
WH— WHY, YES...IT IS SOMETHING I WANTED —BUT HAD GIVEN UP ALL HOPE OF RECEIVING! AS YOU CAN SEE, IT IS JUST SOME TERRY-CLOTH
AS YOU CAN SEE, TERRY LEE, THE SECRET POLICE OF KIEL'S COUNTRY HAVE NOT RELAXED THE WATCH AT THE BUILDING IN WHICH YOUR PRETTY FRIEND IS LIVING! THAT MEANS SHE IS STILL ALIVE!
5-5
Reg. U. S. Pat. Off.: Copyright, 1941, by News Syndicate Co. Inc.
....TRUST BURMA TO WRIGGLE OUT OF TROUBLE! SHE'LL KNOW I AM ALIVE, SINCE WE SENT HER THAT BOLT OF TERRY-CLOTH!
THIS BUILDING ACROSS THE STREET FROM HER HOUSE WILL SERVE AS A WATCHING POST TO FOLLOW HER MOVEMENTS!
SINCE SHE POSSESSES INFORMATION THAT WILL BE USEFUL TO THE BRITISH, WE WHO WORK FOR LONDON WILL HELP YOU GET HER AWAY FROM OUR ENEMIES.... BUT REMEMBER — IF WE SHOULD FIND YOU DANGEROUS — WE CAN BE JUST AS RUTHLESS AS OUR ADVERSARIES!
MILTON CANIFF
THERE'S THAT PUDGY SECRET POLICEMAN GOING INTO BURMA'S PLACE AGAIN! SHE MUST HAVE STALLED HIM, SOMEHOW! NOTHING TO DO NOW BUT WAIT FOR A BREAK — SINCE SHE KNOWS I'M ALIVE AND ON THE JOB!
5-6
Reg. U. S. Pat. Off.: Copyright, 1941, by News Syndicate Co. Inc.
KIEL'S DEAD — BUT TERRY TIPPED ME OFF THAT HE'S IN THERE PITCHIN'.... CAN'T TELL WHAT'S COMING — BUT I'LL HAVE TO PLAY ALONG WITH MR. SNOOPS! HE THINKS I MIGHT FIT A PART IN HIS COPS' AND ROBBERS' GAME!.... HEY! THAT'LL BE SNOOPY NOW!
YOU SEEM REFRESHED SINCE THE THREAT OF EXTINCTION HAS EASED!
NOTHING LIKE A REPRIEVE TO MAKE YOUR HAIR LIE DOWN, I ALWAYS SAY! WHAT DO YOU ALWAYS SAY?
HAVE YOU THOUGHT OVER MY OFFER TO MAKE YOURSELF USEFUL TO MY ORGANIZATION?
I'VE DECIDED TO PLAY BALL WITH YOU.... I LOOK LOUSY IN LILIES!
MILTON CANIFF

NO USE KIDDING MYSELF... I'M ALONE IN OCCUPIED CHINA —IF I DON'T WORK FOR YOUR SECRET POLICE, I'LL END UP IN A RICE FIELD! PLAY THE TUNE — I'LL DANCE!
...VERY SENSIBLE! YOUR FIRST ASSIGNMENT IS READY!
5-7
Reg. U. S. Pat. Off.: Copyright, 1941, by News Syndicate Co. Inc.
WE KNOW THERE MUST HAVE BEEN A BRITISH SPY ABOARD THE RAIDER ON WHICH KIEL DIED... BUT WORSE THAN THAT, WE SUSPECT THAT ONE MAY HAVE CREPT INTO OUR SECRET POLICE UNIT HERE!...
...THE MAN WE SUSPECT HAS NOT SLIPPED UP— BUT HE MIGHT BECOME CARELESS AROUND A BEAUTIFUL WOMAN....
...IT WILL BE ARRANGED FOR YOU TO MEET HIM! YOU WILL GET HIM TO TALK — THEN REPORT YOUR FINDINGS! DURING ALL THIS YOU WILL BE CAREFULLY SHADOWED, OF COURSE!
OH, OF COURSE!... YOU WILL WANT YOUR BOYS AROUND IN CASE YOUR STOOL-PIGEON LAYS AN EGG!
MILTON CANIFF

REMEMBER — OUR AGENTS ARE EVERYWHERE — SO DO NOT ATTEMPT ESCAPE! THE MAN YOU ARE TO MEET WILL BE IN THE RAILROAD STATION! YOU KNOW WHAT TO DO?
SURE! IF I COULDN'T PULL THIS OFF I SHOULD BE SENT BACK TO THE FACTORY FOR A NEW FACE!
5-8
Reg. U. S. Pat. Off.: Copyright, 1941, by News Syndicate Co. Inc.
THAT MUST BE MY GUY! I'LL DO A LITTLE WORRIED PACING TO GIVE HIM A FEW WHIFFS OF PERFUME!
LATER
THE REFUGEE TRAIN FROM SUANTUNG... DO YOU KNOW ANYTHING ABOUT IT?
NO KETCH, MISSY!
OH, DEAR!
MAY I HELP YOU, MISS!
MILTON CANIFF

COULD I BE OF SERVICE, MISS? AS YOU SEE, I SPEAK ENGLISH!
IT'S A PUSH! IF THIS POOR GUY REALLY IS A BRITISH SPY HE SHOULD BE MORE CAREFUL!
OH DEAR ME!
5-9
Reg. U. S. Pat. Off.: Copyright, 1941, by News Syndicate Co. Inc.
OH, THANK YOU, SIR! MY FATHER AND I MUST LEAVE THE COUNTRY! HE WAS TO COME HERE ON THE REFUGEE TRAIN FROM SUANTUNG!
THAT TRAIN HAS BEEN DELAYED BY THE GUERILLA ACTIVITY! I AM SO SORRY!
IT'S SO AWKWARD BEING AN AMERICAN OUT HERE NOW! I AM SO FRIGHTENED WITHOUT FATHER AROUND!... WELL, THANK YOU FOR YOUR KINDNESS!
MILTON CANIFF
...I AM WITH A MERCANTILE FIRM HERE... PERHAPS YOU WOULD FEEL SAFER IF I SAW YOU TO YOUR HOTEL! THE STREETS ARE NOT TOO HEALTHY AT NIGHT!
THERE ARE SO FEW OCCIDENTALS HERE NOW — AND YOU HAVE BEEN SWEET! I SUPPOSE FATHER WOULDN'T MIND MY SPEAKING TO A STRANGER — UNDER THE CIRCUMSTANCES!

...YOU GROW IMPATIENT, MR. TERRY LEE!
CAN'T HELP IT! WE SAW BURMA LEAVE HER PLACE WITH THAT FAT GENT FROM THE SECRET POLICE... BUT WHERE DID SHE GO! WHAT ARE THEY UP TO?
5-10
Reg. U. S. Pat. Off.: Copyright, 1941, by News Syndicate Co. Inc.
WE SHALL KNOW VERY SHORTLY!
BUT HOW? WE CAN'T FOLLOW THEM TOO CLOSELY— IT WOULD LOOK SUSPICIOUS!
QUITE SO! FOR THAT REASON WE PURSUE A DIFFERENT COURSE! ...THIS SECRET POLICE CHIEF MUST EMPLOY SERVANTS — SO WE HAVE WORKED ONE OF OUR MEN INTO HIS HOUSEHOLD!...
MEANWHILE...
THE AMERICAN WOMAN MADE HER CONTACT AT THE STATION — AS ORDERED!
GOOD! NOW WE SHALL SEE IF THESE YANKEES ARE AS CLEVER AS THEY THINK!
MILTON CANIFF

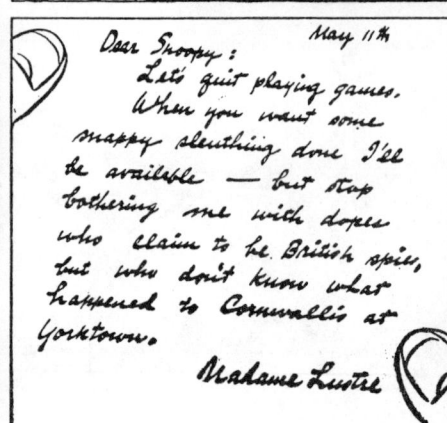

TERRY AND THE PIRATES
by MILTON CANIFF

Panel 1: DO NOT BECOME IMPATIENT, MR. TERRY LEE! YOUR BEAUTIFUL FRIEND KNOWS YOU ARE WORKING ON HER BEHALF.... SHE IS SO CLOSELY GUARDED BY SECRET POLICE SHE HAS PROBABLY ALLOWED THEM TO THINK SHE IS FRIENDLY TO THEIR CAUSE... TO SAVE HER OWN LIFE!

Panel 2: WELL, HERE GOES!...OLD SNOOPY ARRANGED FOR THIS GUY TO MEET ME 'ACCIDENTALLY'! THEY SUSPECT HIM OF BEING A BRITISH SPY!...I'M SUPPOSED TO GET THE DOPE—AND SINCE MY OWN NECK'S IN A SLING I GUESS I'LL HAVE TO MAKE A STAB AT IT!

WON'T YOU COME TO MY PLACE FOR A BITE OF SUPPER?

DELIGHTED!

Panel 3: HEY! WH—

JUST BOLTING THE DOOR!... MUST ACT QUICKLY! ARE THERE HIDDEN MICROPHONES IN THIS ROOM?

Panel 4: WHY, NO! I COMBED THE PLACE TO FIND OUT!...WHY DO YOU LOOK IN THE CLOSETS!

WE MUST NOT BE OVERHEARD!...THEY SENT YOU TO FIND OUT IF I AM A BRITISH SPY! WELL, I AM!

Panel 5: HOLY CATS! WHY ARE YOU TELLING ME—WHEN YOU KNOW I'M GETTING PAID TO EXPOSE YOU, IF POSSIBLE?

I KNOW THEY ARE HOLDING YOU BY THREATENING YOU WITH DEATH IF YOU TRY TO ESCAPE WITH KIEL'S SECRETS!

Panel 6: I MUST STAY ON HERE—BUT I CAN GET YOU TO HONGKONG!.... YOU MUST WRITE A REPORT SAYING I AM NOT A BRITISH SPY—THAT WILL STOP THEIR SUSPICIONS! THEN I WILL SMUGGLE YOU ABOARD MY REGULAR COURIER BOAT—A FAKE FISHING JUNK—WHICH CONTACTS A BRITISH SHIP AT SEA!...IN RETURN YOU WILL TELL WHAT YOU KNOW TO OUR HONGKONG GARRISON!

Panel 7: SWELL! AND I HOPE YOU BRITISH BEAT THESE GUYS LIKE CORNWALLIS TOOK YORKTOWN!

WE'LL DO THAT! I'LL LEAVE, NOW! SEND YOUR GOOD REPORT—THEN I'LL CALL FOR YOU TO GO ABOARD THE BOAT!

Panel 8: WHAT LUCK?

IT WAS SIMPLE, EXCELLENCY! THE WOMAN SHOULD BE SHOT! THE MOMENT I TOLD HER I WAS A BRITISH SPY SHE LEAPED AT THE CHANCE TO GET AWAY! SHE CANNOT BE TRUSTED!

Panel 9: BAH! THESE WOMEN ARE NEVER AS CLEVER AS THEY THINK! WHEN HER INCRIMINATING REPORT ARRIVES I SHALL GO AND SHOOT HER AS A COMPLETE NUISANCE!

THIS MAY BE HER MESSAGE NOW!

Panel 10: I HAVE TO LAUGH WHEN I THINK HOW EAGERLY SHE BELIEVED MY STORY! MY STUDY OF ENGLISH PROVED VALUABLE TONIGHT! DOES SHE SPEAK WELL OF ME?

...READ IT FOR YOURSELF!

Panel 11: May 11th

Dear Snoopy:

Let's quit playing games. When you want some snappy sleuthing done I'll be available — but stop bothering me with dopes who claim to be British spies, but who don't know what happened to Cornwallis at Yorktown.

Madame Lustre

WAKE UP, MR. TERRY LEE! OUR AGENT WHO WORKS AS A SERVANT WITH THE SECRET POLICE OF KIEL'S PEOPLE HAS MADE A REPORT ON YOUR BURMA!.... IT SEEMS THOSE CHAPS FORCED HER TO WORK FOR THEM....THEN TRIED TO TEST HER INTEGRITY...
5-12
Reg. U. S. Pat. Off. Copyright, 1941, by News Syndicate Co. Inc.
THEY HAD HER MEET A MAN THEY SAID WAS SUSPECTED OF BEING A BRITISH SPY! SHE WAS TO EXPOSE HIM, IF POSSIBLE! TO HER SURPRISE, HE SAID AT ONCE HE REALLY WAS AN ENGLISHMAN...
...HE OFFERED TO HELP HER ESCAPE IF SHE WOULD NOT GIVE HIM UP!...BURMA AGREED AND SENT HIM AWAY, SAYING SHE HOPED HIS BRITISH FRIENDS WON —THE WAY CORNWALLIS DID AT YORKTOWN... AND HE DID NOT CORRECT HER!
...SO SHE WROTE A REPORT TO THE CHIEF, TELLING HIM NOT TO ANNOY HER WITH ALLEGED BRITISH SPIES WHO DIDN'T KNOW ENGLISH HISTORY! AMUSING, EH?
AMAZING! WHAT I CAN'T GET IS HOW BURMA KNEW WHAT HAPPENED TO ANYONE YOU HAVE TO LEARN ABOUT BY READING A BOOK!
MILTON CANIFF

I KNOW YOU HAVE OTHER PROBLEMS BESIDES HELPING ME GET BURMA AWAY FROM THOSE SECRET COPS.... BUT I'D LIKE TO HAVE SOME WAY TO KEEP IN DIRECT TOUCH WITH HER!...
5-13
Reg. U. S. Pat. Off. Copyright, 1941, by News Syndicate Co. Inc.
YOUR BEAUTY IS CLOSELY GUARDED, MR. TERRY LEE! IF YOU HIT ON SOME PLAN WE WILL GIVE YOU ALL ASSISTANCE — IN RETURN FOR THE INFORMATION SHE MAY GIVE OUR EMPLOYERS IN LONDON!
BOY— IF I COULD JUST SIT AND WRITE HER A NOTE ON THIS TYPEWRITER... OR IF SHE COULD WRITE TO ME IN SOME SORT OF CODE....HEY!..
...WE HAVE THAT OBSERVATION POST ON THE ROOF ACROSS FROM HER PLACE.... IT MIGHT BE POSSIBLE!... COULD YOU CALL IN YOUR TYPEWRITER REPAIR MAN?
MILTON CANIFF

WHAT'S ALL THE COMMOTION? I THOUGHT YOU WERE PLANTED TO GUARD ME!... ARE YOU RUNNING A BOOKIE JOINT HERE IN THE HALL?
SORRY, MISS! THIS BOY SAYS HE HAS A TYPEWRITER YOU SENT TO BE REPAIRED! I HAVE ORDERS TO LET NOTHING REACH YOU!
5-14
Reg. U. S. Pat. Off. Copyright, 1941, by News Syndicate Co. Inc.
YIPPEE! THIS IS TERRY'S DOING!
WELL, LET ME HAVE MY TYPEWRITER.. YOU START TO WORRY AFTER I WRITE SOMETHING! ...THINK I RAISE PIGEONS?
I'VE LOOKED IT OVER... GUESS THERE'S NOTHING YOU COULD HIDE ANYWHERE!
THAT DOPE ON THE DOOR IS TOO RIGHT! WHAT CAN YOU HIDE IN A TYPEWRITER THAT WOULD HELP BURMA AT THIS POINT? —AND YET... THERE MUST BE SOMETHING!
MILTON CANIFF
THEY'VE SEARCHED ALL MY THINGS FOR A MEANS OF SIGNALING TO THE OUTSIDE ...TERRY MUST HAVE GUESSED THAT AND SENT THIS MACHINE! —BUT WHAT HAPPENS?.... I'LL RUN OVER THE KEYS AND....YOW!

5-15
Reg. U. S. Pat. Off. Copyright, 1941, by
THE TYPEWRITER TERRY SENT—AS IF IT WERE MINE COMING FROM THE REPAIR SHOP — IT WRITES IN MORSE CODE!...THERE ARE TEMPORARY CAPS ON THE KEYS — SO I CAN GET THE CODE—THEN TOSS 'EM AWAY!...BUT WHAT THEN?
TERRY MEANS FOR ME TO SIGNAL... AND FROM THE WINDOW, OBVIOUSLY! —BUT HOW?... A FLASHLIGHT AT NIGHT IS THE ONLY WAY!
HE MUST KNOW I HAVE NO FLASHLIGHT— SO HE WOULD SMUGGLE ONE... AND THE ONLY POSSIBLE PLACE FOR THAT WOULD BE ... LET'S SEE ...IN THE ROLLER!
MILTON CANIFF

HOCUS MALOKUS! TERRY SENT ME A MORSE CODE AND FLASHLIGHT — SO I CAN LET HIM KNOW WHAT'S UP!... BUT I'LL HAVE TO BE CAREFUL .... THAT'LL BE OLD SNOOPS AT THE DOOR NOW!
5-16
Reg. U. S. Pat. Off.; Copyright, 1941, by News Syndicate Co. Inc.
...I WILL NOT GO INTO THE INCIDENT OF THE MAN WE SENT TO TRIP YOU! HE IS A FOOL — AND YOU ARE CLEVER! I HAVE A LEGITIMATE ASSIGNMENT FOR YOU!
OKAY, POPS! ...I'LL DO YOUR LITTLE STICKY JOBS!.. GOT MORE HEELS IN YOUR CLIQUE?
SOMETIMES YOUR USE OF THE AMERICAN IDIOM IS CONFUSING — BUT I UNDERSTAND WHAT YOU MEAN!...
THERE IS A CERTAIN COLONEL WOLFF — AN ENGINEER SUPERVISING THE BUILDING OF A DAM IN OCCUPIED CHINA ....
THIS MAN IS HIGHLY CAPABLE — BUT HE IS NOT FULLY APPRECIATIVE OF THE POLITICAL ASPECTS OF THE NEW ORDER IN OUR COUNTRY!
YOU MEAN YOU HAVE NOTHING ON THIS GUY — AND YOU WANT ME TO GET SOMETHING ON HIM... PREFERABLY LIPSTICK!
MILTON CANIFF
SO THERE'S AN ENGINEER NAMED WOLFF BUILDING SOME LONESOME DAM! I'M TO GO THERE AND GET ENOUGH ON HIM SO YOU CAN KEEP HIM IN LINE!
EXACTLY! YOU WILL POSE AS MRS. KAMP, WIFE OF ONE OF OUR SECRET POLICE AGENTS WHO STOPPED WITH WOLFF ON HIS WAY TO THE INTERIOR!
5-17
Reg. U. S. Pat. Off.; Copyright, 1941, by News Syndicate Co. Inc.
IT WILL BE LOGICAL THAT YOU WERE TO MEET YOUR HUSBAND THERE — AND MUST WAIT!
— BUT WHAT ABOUT AN AMERICAN BEING THE WIFE OF ONE OF YOUR "NEW ORDER" BOYS!
HE MARRIED YOU IN — SAY — SHANGHAI... BEFORE THE WAR!...
TO SAVE ME FROM THE FATE OF BEING A CITIZEN OF A DEMOCRACY?
WHY — AH — YES! I SEE THAT YOU ARE BEGINNING TO UNDERSTAND THE WISDOM OF OUR GREAT LEADER — WHO HAS ---
HOLD IT, POPS! I DON'T DRINK THE PAIN-KILLER, JUST BECAUSE YOU FORCED ME TO BE PART OF THE MEDICINE SHOW.... POLITICALLY SPEAKING... YOU GO YOUR WAY — I'LL GO MINE... ♫ AND I'LL BE IN SCOTLAND BEFORE YOU ♫
MILTON CANIFF
TERRY AND THE PIRATES
by MILTON CANIFF
LET'S NOT KID EACH OTHER!... I HAVE TO TAKE YOUR ORDERS BECAUSE THERE'S NO CHOICE! BUT DON'T EXPECT ME TO ACT SYMPATHETIC TO YOUR CAUSE!
OF COURSE! I ONLY TRIED TO TEST YOU BEFORE! YOUR NEW ASSIGNMENT IS QUITE SERIOUS BUSINESS! REPEAT YOUR ORDERS!
OKAY! THERE'S AN ENGINEER NAMED WOLFF ACTING AS THE TECHNICAL ADVISOR ON A DAM THE INVADER IS BUILDING IN OCCUPIED CHINA!
...THIS WOLFF IS A GOOD ENGINEER ... BUT HE DOESN'T ACT ENTHUSIASTIC ENOUGH ABOUT YOUR COUNTRY'S AMBITIONS! YOU THINK HE WILL GO SO FAR ON HIS ABILITY THAT THE SECRET POLICE MUST HAVE SOMETHING ON HIM — TO WHIP HIM INTO LINE!...
THAT'S PUTTING IT CRUDELY! — BUT GO ON!
LOOK WHO'S GETTING DELICATE! .... ANYHOW, A SECRET POLICEMAN NAMED KAMP RECENTLY STOPPED AT WOLFF'S PLACE ON HIS WAY TO THE INTERIOR!... I AM TO GO TO WOLFF'S PLACE AS IF I AM MRS. KAMP, EXPECTING TO FIND MY HUSBAND THERE! THIS KAMP IS SUPPOSED TO HAVE MARRIED ME IN SHANGHAI — BEFORE THE WAR... WHICH EXPLAINS MY BEING AMERICAN!
WHILE I AM SUPPOSEDLY WAITING FOR THIS KAMP TO RETURN AND PICK ME UP, I AM TO PLAY ON WOLFF'S LONELINESS AND GET HIM TO TALK FREELY WITH ME — HOPING HE'LL SPILL HIS REAL THOUGHTS!... THEN I'LL REPORT THEM TO YOU — SO YOU CAN SLAP HIM DOWN IF HE DOESN'T CLICK HIS HEELS LOUDLY ENOUGH!

QUITE RIGHT!... AND I AM SENDING THESE TWO MEN WITH YOU! THEY WILL POSE AS NEW ASSISTANTS TO WOLFF! REALLY THEY WILL KEEP AN EYE ON YOU!
A SPY ON A SPY IS A SPY IS A SPY ON A SPY... SOUNDS LIKE A DIZZY OPERA I HEARD ABOUT ONCE!
...I'LL FINISH PACKING! DON'T YOU BOYS DISCUSS ANY SECRETS IN FRONT OF THE CANARY! HE MAY BE AN ENGLISH SPARROW IN DISGUISE!
GOTTA WORK FAST!... LUCKY TERRY SMUGGLED THIS FLASHLIGHT AND MORSE CODE TO ME!... HE'S ON THE ROOF ACROSS THE STREET! HE'LL HAVE TO FOLLOW ME SOME WAY IF WE'RE BOTH TO GET OUT OF THIS CRAZY MESS!
LATER...
I SUPPOSE YOU TWO WILL RIDE IN A DIFFERENT PART OF THE TRAIN — SO THIS WOLFF WON'T HAVE THE SLIGHTEST IDEA WE TRAVELED TOGETHER!
QUITE SO!
... WHY ARE ALL THOSE CHINESE BEING LOADED INTO BOX CARS ON OUR TRAIN?
THEY GO TO LABOR ON WOLFF'S DAM!
5-18
...THE AMERICAN WOMAN IS SETTLED IN THE OTHER CAR! THE COMMANDER HOPES SHE MAY BE ABLE TO CAUSE THIS COLONEL WOLFF TO REVEAL HIS LACK OF LOYALTY TO THE NEW ORDER!
THESE AMERICAN FEMALES HAVE A CERTAIN TYPE OF ARTIFICIAL BEAUTY ... WHICH MAY BE ATTRACTIVE TO SUCH A PERSON AS WOLFF!
5-19
Reg. U. S. Pat. Off.: Copyright, 1941, by News Syndicate Co. Inc.
QUITE POSSIBLY — IF HE IS NOT WHOLEHEARTEDLY DEVOTED TO THE DOCTRINES OF THE LEADER!... WEAK MEN ARE DRAWN TO THE WOMEN OF THE DECADENT DEMOCRACIES!
QUITE SO!
I AM HAPPY THAT WE ARE BEING SENT AS ASSISTANTS TO WOLFF.... IN ORDER TO SUPERVISE THE WOMAN'S CAMPAIGN! I REJOICE THAT MY TRAINING KEEPS ME FROM NOTICING HER BLATANT PRETTINESS!
OH, ABSOLUTELY!
MILTON CANIFF
A GUARD IN EACH VESTIBULE OF THIS TUXEDO JUNCTION LOCAL... COULDN'T JUMP THE JERKER IF I WANTED TO! ... BESIDES, TERRY'S UP FRONT IN A BOX CAR WITH HIS HAIR BLACKENED — SO THEY'LL TAKE HIM FOR ONE OF THE RUSSIAN REFUGEE WORKMEN GOING TO THIS DAM WOLFF IS BUILDING!
5-20
GOT TO KEEP IN TOUCH WITH THE KID... TRAIN'S STOPPING!... HE'S SURE TO COME BY THIS WINDOW WITH THE WORK GANG! MUST LEAVE HIM A HINT ABOUT HOW TO FIND ME AT WOLFF'S HOUSE!.... ...THIS MIGHT WORK!
Reg. U. S. Pat. Off.: Copyright, 1941, by News Syndicate Co. Inc.
THE SOLDIERS SEEM TO THINK I'M OKAY AS A REFUGEE WORKMAN!.... HOPE BURMA GIVES ME A SIGNAL — SO I CAN GET IN TOUCH WITH HER LATER! SHE MUST BE ON ONE OF THOSE PASSENGER CARS!
THERE SHE IS... WITH AN "X" ON THE WINDOW IN LIPSTICK! WHAT'S THE PITCH?...OH! I GET IT!..."X MARKS MY ROOM"! THAT'S THE WAY I'LL KNOW HER QUARTERS WHEN SHE ARRIVES AT THE DAM!
MILTON CANIFF

HERE GOES BURMA INTO HER ACT TO TRY TO TRIP THIS POOR GOOF WOLFF... SO THE SECRET POLICE CAN BOOT HIM INTO LINE!... GOT TO GET OFF AND LOOK INNOCENT AND PUZZLED! ...THEN SETTLE FOR HALF!
5-21
Reg. U. S. Pat. Off.; Copyright, 1941, by News Syndicate Co. Inc.
THAT MUST BE WOLFF THE SECRET POLICE GORILLAS ARE SLIPPING THE GRIP TO! ...I'LL WANDER BY LIKE A LOVING WIFE LOOKING FOR HER HUSBAND!... HOPE THIS WOLFF ISN'T TOO MUCH OF A ZOMBIE!
OH, DEAR!
COULD I HELP YOU, MISS?
WELL, PRESS MY BLUE TAFFETA, MOM! ... WE MAY HAVE SOMETHING HERE!
MILTON CANIFF

YOU SEEM DISTRESSED, MADAME! MAY I HELP?
OH, THANK YOU! IT'S SO NICE TO FIND ONE WHO SPEAKS ENGLISH! I AM MRS. KAMP!
5-22
Reg. U. S. Pat. Off.; Copyright, 1941, by News Syndicate Co. Inc.
I WAS TO MEET MY HUSBAND HERE... HE WAS STOPPING WITH A COLONEL WOLFF!
I AM COLONEL WOLFF... BUT YOUR HUSBAND HAS GONE TO THE INTERIOR!
OH, HEAVENS! I RECEIVED NO MESSAGE! WHAT CAN I DO?
NO DOUBT YOUR HUSBAND HOPED TO RETURN BEFORE NOW...
RATHER THAN MAKE THE TRIP BACK ALONE, YOU MUST ACCEPT MY POOR HOSPITALITY UNTIL KAMP JOINS YOU!
OH, I DON'T KNOW IF I SHOULD....
OH, BROTHER, IF YOU FALL FOR THIS SCHMALTZ YOU DESERVE WHAT'S COMING!
MILTON CANIFF

YOU SHOULD NOT BE CONCERNED ABOUT STOPPING AT MY PLACE UNTIL YOUR HUSBAND RETURNS, MADAME KAMP! MY TWO NEW ASSISTANTS WILL BE THERE AS WELL!
OH! THEN OF COURSE I SHALL BE HAPPY TO ACCEPT, COLONEL WOLFF! I DO HATE TO RETURN TO THE CITY WITH THE WAR GOING ON!
5-23
Reg. U. S. Pat. Off.; Copyright, 1941, by News Syndicate Co. Inc.
WE RARELY USE THE MILITARY TITLES HERE, MADAME KAMP! THE GOVERNMENT OF OCCUPIED CHINA DOESN'T LIKE IT KNOWN THAT OCCIDENTAL SOLDIERS ARE SUPERVISING ITS ENGINEERING PROJECTS... YOU WILL UNDERSTAND, I'M SURE!
OH, YES, I DO UNDERSTAND! BEING BORN AN AMERICAN, I SOMETIMES FORGET SUCH DETAILS ABOUT THE NEW ORDER!
MY HUSBAND HAS TOLD ME WHAT A WONDERFUL ENGINEER YOU ARE, MR. WOLFF! HE THINKS IT IS A SHAME THE HIGH COMMAND KEEPS YOU OUT HERE — INSTEAD OF IN SOME BIG POST!
THAT IS VERY KIND OF YOUR HUSBAND... BUT I PERFORM MY DUTY AS ORDERED BY MY SUPERIORS!
MILTON CANIFF

THIS WOLFF PLAYS 'EM CLOSE TO THE VEST!... SEEMS LIKE A DECENT EGG!... IF THOSE TWO HAPPINESS BOYS WEREN'T AROUND I WOULDN'T HAVE TO TRY TO PRY INTO HIS POLITICAL OPINIONS!
5-24
Reg. U. S. Pat. Off.; Copyright, 1941, by News Syndicate Co. Inc.
THEY'LL WANT A REPORT... BUT TERRY AND I MUST BUST AWAY BEFORE THE SHOWDOWN! THE KID WILL BE OUT WITH THE WORK GANG AT THE DAM WAITING FOR A SIGNAL!... HOPE HE GOT THE "X" IDEA AT THE TRAIN...
NOT SO TOUGH TO SLIP BY THE INVADER GARRISON AT THE DAM! GOTTA CONTACT BURMA TO PLAN A FADE-OUT!... WONDER WHICH IS HER ROOM IN WOLFF'S HOUSE?
CURTAINS JUST CLOSED AT ONE OF THE WINDOWS... NOW THEY'RE OPENING... NOW CLOSING... LONG FLASH... TWO SHORTS... ANOTHER LONG! THE LETTER "X" IN MORSE! "X" MARKS HER ROOM AGAIN! WE'RE RIDIN' NOW!
MILTON CANIFF

Reg. U. S. Pat. Off.: Copyright, 1941, by News Syndicate Co. Inc.
TERRY AND THE PIRATES
by MILTON CANIFF
SINCE YOU ARE AN AMERICAN, YOU POSSIBLY PREFER BEING CALLED MRS. KAMP!
WHY – AH – AS YOU LIKE! IT IS SO DISAPPOINTING TO FIND THAT MY HUSBAND HAS BEEN HERE AND GONE! AND YOU SAY HE WON'T RETURN FOR SOME TIME, MR. WOLFF?
NO! WHEN HE PASSED THROUGH HERE HE WAS ON SOME SORT OF SECRET MISSION IN UNOCCUPIED CHINA! I KNOW YOU MUST FEEL TERRIBLY LET DOWN!
IT IS SO KIND OF YOU TO INVITE ME TO WAIT HERE FOR HIM! I FEEL RATHER UNEASY IN THE CITIES ... WITH THE WAR GOING ON!
I UNDERSTAND! ... IT IS VERY LONELY IN THIS OUT-OF-THE-WAY PLACE! IT WILL BE A PLEASURE TO HAVE YOUR COMPANY!
I NOTICED THE TWO YOUNG MEN ON THE TRAIN ... THEY ARE TO BE YOUR ASSISTANTS HERE?
YES! I AM SUPERVISING THE CONSTRUCTION OF THIS DAM ... BUT MY SUPERIORS FELT THAT I NEEDED HELP ... YOU KNOW HOW IT IS!
OH, YES! SOMETIMES I GET SO ANGRY WITH THE HIGH COMMAND ... ESPECIALLY WHEN MY HUSBAND IS SENT ON THESE TERRIBLE TRIPS! DON'T YOU THINK THE LEADERS OVERDO THINGS SOMETIMES?
I AM ONLY AN ENGINEER, MADAME! I OBEY MY ORDERS WITHOUT A QUESTION!
OH, OF COURSE, YOU MUST! THAT'S WHAT MY HUSBAND ALWAYS SAYS! I WISH HE WEREN'T IN POLICE WORK — MAYBE WE COULD GO TO THE UNITED STATES! WOULD YOU LIKE TO GO TO AMERICA, MR. WOLFF?
... IN MY PROFESSION IT DOESN'T MATTER, MADAME! I AM AN ENGINEER ... WHEREVER I LIVE!
IT'S RATHER LATE! IF YOU DON'T MIND I THINK I'LL RETIRE! GOOD NIGHT, MR. WOLFF!
GOOD NIGHT, MRS. KAMP!
NEAR DAWN THERE IS A SCRATCHING SOUND AT BURMA'S WINDOW ....
SO FAR SO GOOD, TERRY! GLAD WE GOT TOGETHER FOR A SECOND TO ARRANGE THESE SIGNALS!
I GOT A JOB AT THE DAM! THERE ARE PLENTY OF RUSSIAN REFUGEES HERE ... THE BOSSES THINK I'M ONE OF THEM!
HOW'S IT GOING WITH YOU? WHAT ABOUT THOSE TWO GENTS WHO WERE WITH YOU ON THE TRAIN?
THEY HAVE THE ROOM ACROSS THE HALL! CAN'T TELL MUCH ABOUT THIS WOLFF GUY! I'M GIVING HIM THE OLD HOCUS-MALOCUS ABOUT WAITING HERE FOR MY ALLEGED HUSBAND!
OKAY! THERE'S A SMALL INVADER GARRISON HERE GUARDING THE DAM ... BUT WE'LL FIND A WAY TO DITCH THEM! ... 'BYE!
S'LONG, HONEY!
5-25

BURMA SEEMS SAFE ENOUGH AT WOLFF'S HOUSE... IF THOSE TWO SECRET POLICE STOOGES WEREN'T THERE, TOO, WE MIGHT MAKE A BREAK FROM HERE! MY JOB NOW IS TO ACT LIKE A RUSSIAN REFUGEE AND KEEP A JOB ON THIS DAM!
5-26
Reg. U. S. Pat. Off.: Copyright, 1941, by News Syndicate Co. Inc.
SHOULDN'T BE SO HARD... WITH MY HAIR BLACKENED... THERE ARE PLENTY OF RUSSIANS HERE IN THE CONSTRUCTION GANG! I SHOULD BE IN THE PLUSH IF I KEEP MY MOUTH SHUT — MAYBE THEY'LL THINK I'M JUST A SOUR PUSS WHO DOESN'T LIKE TO MIX WITH PEOPLE!
HOLY CATS!...
HERE COMES ONE OF THE INVADER STRAW-BOSSES — TALKING TO EACH MAN! ...WITH ONE OF THE RUSSIANS AS AN INTERPRETER!!!
MILTON CANIFF

I BLACKED MY HAIR THINKING I COULD POSE AS ONE OF THE RUSSIAN REFUGEES ON THE DAM PROJECT... NOW, HERE COMES THE INVADER STRAW-BOSS... WITH ONE OF THE RUSSIANS ACTING AS INTERPRETER...
5-27
Reg. U. S. Pat. Off.: Copyright, 1941, by News Syndicate Co. Inc.
CAN'T UNDERSTAND A WORD... BUT HE MUST BE ASKING MY NAME, AGE AND STUFF FOR THE PAYROLL...
PAWNEE IROQUOIS COMANCHE NAVAJO! ... PUEBLO SHAWNEE SIOUX SEMINOLE? ...PASSAMAQUODDY WITH A FLOY FLOY!!
A STRANGE DIALECT! HE MUST BE FROM SOME REMOTE SIBERIAN TRIBE!
I HAVE NO TIME FOR ACCENTS! FROM NOW ON HE IS NUMBER 364!
364
MILTON CANIFF

THIS WOLFF BABY IS NO FOOL! THAT SECRET POLICE CHIEF WANTS ME TO GET WOLFF TO SAY SOMETHING CRITICAL ABOUT HIS GOVERNMENT — SO THEY CAN HOLD IT OVER HIM LATER... BUT HE'S CAGEY AS A ZOO!
SOME ONE KNOCKING... MAYBE WOLFF WANTS TO TALK, AFTER ALL!
5-28
Reg. U. S. Pat. Off.: Copyright, 1941, by News Syndicate Co. Inc.
GOOD EVENING! I CLOSE THE DOOR FOR FEAR COLONEL WOLFF SHALL BECOME SUSPICIOUS
OH, NO! HE'D JUST THINK YOU CAME TO FIX THE VACUUM CLEANER! WHAT'S ON YOUR MIND, IF ANY?
MY SUPERIOR AWAITS A REPORT ON COLONEL WOLFF!
DON'T RUSH ME, SON! DO YOU THINK THIS WOLFF WAS BORN YESTERDAY?
NO, MISS! HIS RECORD SHOWS HE WAS BORN JANUARY 31, 1902
YOU'LL PARDON ME IF I SHAKE! ... ANY KIND OF DOPE AFFECTS ME THIS WAY!
MILTON CANIFF

HIS EXCELLENCY, MY SUPERIOR IN THE SECRET POLICE, EXPECTS YOU TO EXERT YOUR CHARMS UPON COLONEL WOLFF IN ORDER TO ACHIEVE OUR PURPOSE!
...I SUPPOSE ONE OF YOUR MOB IS IN A JAM IF HIS RECORD SHOWS HE SAILED FOR AN AMERICAN GIRL...
5-29
Reg. U. S. Pat. Off.: Copyright, 1941, by News Syndicate Co. Inc.
I GUESS THEY THINK HE'D GO A LITTLE HAYWIRE... IF THE GAL HAD ENOUGH OF THAT OLD FREQUENCY MODULATION!
AND IF SHE EVER GOT HER ARMS AROUND HIM — SHE COULD TELL HIS SUPERIORS ... AND GET HIM SENT TO A CONCENTRATION CAMP!!
THAT'S THE FIRST TIME BURMA EVER DID THAT TO GET RID OF A GUY!
MILTON CANIFF

OUR SUPERIOR WILL GROW MOST IMPATIENT FOR A REPORT ON COLONEL WOLFF! DID YOU SPEAK TO THE WOMAN?
YES! YOU WILL PUT THE REPORT INTO CODE AS I DICTATE!
5-30
Reg. U. S. Pat. Off.: Copyright, 1941, by News Syndicate Co. Inc.
...THE WOMAN RELATES THAT COLONEL WOLFF HAS NOT AS YET REVEALED A TREASONABLE ATTITUDE... HOWEVER, SHE HOPES SOON TO EXERT ENOUGH FEMININE APPEAL TO CAUSE HIM TO CONFIDE IN HER....
...THIS DELAY IS UNFORTUNATE — BUT THE WOMAN HAS DEMONSTRATED TO ME THE TECHNIQUE SHE WILL USE ON WOLFF... AND THERE IS LITTLE DOUBT OF EVENTUAL SUCCESS...
MILTON CANIFF

YOU MUST NOT MISUNDERSTAND WHAT I SAID IN THE REPORT TO OUR SUPERIOR ABOUT THE WOMAN DEMONSTRATING HER ALLURE TO ME!
OH, OF COURSE NOT!... THE REPORT IS IN CODE... READY TO GO TO THE RAILWAY STATION!
5-31
Reg. U. S. Pat. Off.: Copyright, 1941, by News Syndicate Co. Inc.
REMEMBER! YOU ARE BEING PAID TO CARRY THIS DIRECTLY TO THE CHIEF ATTENDANT OF THE FIVE O'CLOCK TRAIN AT THE STATION!
MILTON CANIFF

Reg. U. S. Pat. Off.: Copyright, 1941, by News Syndicate Co. Inc.
TERRY AND THE PIRATES by MILTON CANIFF
THERE ARE SOME CHINESE GUERILLAS IN THE LABOR GANG AT THE DAM, BURMA! OUR BEST CHANCE TO GET AWAY IS THROUGH THEM! ...THE INVADER BOSSES STILL THINK I'M A RUSSIAN REFUGEE!
GOOD! THIS WOLFF GUY IS A DECENT EGG! HE THINKS I'M MRS. KAMP — WIFE OF A SECRET POLICEMAN WHO'S TO MEET ME HERE! ... BUT THOSE TWO STOOGES WHO CAME HERE WITH ME KEEP A BIG EYE ON EVERYTHING I DO! I CAN'T STALL THEM LONG! ... NOISE IN THE HALL — BETTER BEAT IT, TERRY!
OKAY! I'LL SLIP BACK TO THE DAM WHEN THEY CHANGE SENTRIES!
ON YOUR FEET! ATTENTION!!

STRAIGHTEN YOUR BACKS, DUMB-HEADS!... DO YOU KNOW THAT THIS IS A MILITARY ASSIGNMENT, EVEN THOUGH WE DO NOT WEAR ARMY UNIFORMS? DO YOU KNOW THAT I AM A COLONEL OF ENGINEERS... YOUR SUPERIOR OFFICER?
YES, SIR!
...DID I ORDER YOU TO PEEP AT MADAME KAMP'S DOOR — LIKE A PAIR OF MAIL-ORDER DETECTIVES?
NO, SIR!
..THEN AS LONG AS YOU ARE UNDER MY COMMAND YOU WILL PERFORM YOUR DUTIES AS ENGINEERS!...YOU MAY WRITE YOUR SUPERIOR IN THE SECRET POLICE THAT I EXPECT MY MEN TO DO ONLY ONE THING AT A TIME!... YOU WILL STAND AT ATTENTION UNTIL DAYLIGHT!
NEXT DAY
GOOD MORNING, MR. WOLFF! YOU SEEM MOODY!
...I WAS JUST THINKING HOW OFTEN PEOPLE TRY TO APPEAR TO THE WORLD IN A CERTAIN LIGHT — THEN REVEAL THEIR TRUE SELVES BY FORGETTING SOME SIMPLE PART OF THEIR ASSUMED CHARACTER!
... FOR INSTANCE ... IF I DID NOT KNOW YOU WERE MRS. KAMP... YOU COULD PRETEND YOU WERE MARRIED — BUT I WOULD IMMEDIATELY BE SUSPICIOUS, BECAUSE I HAVE NEVER SEEN YOU WEAR A WEDDING RING!!!
I USUALLY CARRY IT AROUND MY NECK! ... AS YOU SAY — IT IS SO EASY TO FORGET THINGS — SOMETIMES!
6-1
WHERE IS THAT KITCHEN BOY?
HIM JUST COME IN, MASTER! ...WILL SEND!
6-2
Reg. U. S. Pat. Off.: Copyright, 1941, by News Syndicate Co. Inc.
WHERE HAVE YOU BEEN?
HAVE SISTER SICK IN VILLAGE, MASTER! MADE PLENTY SUDDEN GO!
EXCELLENT! THE BOY GOT OUR REPORT ON WOLFF TO THE RAILROAD!
MILTON CANIFF
THE WAY SOME OF THE CHINESE IN THIS CONSTRUCTION CREW GET TOGETHER, I KNOW THEY MUST BE HATCHING A SCHEME... BUT AS LONG AS THEY THINK I'M A RUSSIAN REFUGEE THEY WON'T GIVE ME A HINT OF THEIR PLANS!...
6-3
Reg. U. S. Pat. Off.: Copyright, 1941, by News Syndicate Co. Inc.
...POSSIBLY THEY ARE TRYING TO SABOTAGE THIS DAM!.. THAT WOULD BE THE BREAK TO GET BURMA AWAY FROM THOSE SECRET POLICE GENTS!...
...MAYBE IT'S JUST AS WELL THEY DO THINK I'M ONE OF THE RUSSIANS!... THEN I WON'T GET IN A JAM IF THEIR STUNT GOES ASKEW!
PATIENCE, MY FRIENDS! THE ONE CALLED WOLFF WILL SLIP A SINGLE TIME... THEN OUR CHANCE WILL COME!
...WHAT OF THE RUSSIANS?
WE WILL PROTECT THEM AS LONG AS POSSIBLE! BEYOND THAT THEY MUST LOOK TO THEIR OWN SAFETY!
MILTON CANIFF

OH, HELLO, MR. WOLFF!... I-I-COULDN'T SLEEP! WHERE ARE YOUR TWO ASSISTANTS?
THEY'VE GONE TO BED, MRS. KAMP! WOULD YOU CARE TO SIT DOWN?
6-4
Reg. U. S. Pat. Off.: Copyright, 1941, by News Syndicate Co. Inc.
THANK YOU!.... HOW IS THE DAM GETTING ON?
IF YOU DON'T MIND... LET'S STOP PLAYING YOUR PRETTY LITTLE GAME!
WHY-- WHATEVER DO YOU MEAN, MR. WOLFF?
OW! WHERE DID I SLIP?
I THINK IT WOULD BE BEST TO LOCK THE DOORS AND WINDOWS BEFORE WE TALK ABOUT IT, MRS. KAMP!
MILTON CANIFF

WHY ARE YOU LOCKING THE DOORS AND WINDOWS, MR. WOLFF?
BECAUSE I AM WEARY OF THE CHARMING GAME YOU'VE BEEN PLAYING, MRS. KAMP — AND I DO NOT WISH TO BE OVERHEARD WHEN I ADD UP THE SCORE!
6-5
Reg. U. S. Pat. Off.: Copyright, 1941, by News Syndicate Co. Inc.
BUT THIS IS ABSURD!... WHEN I TELL MY HUSBAND OF THIS--
YOU MAY DROP ALL THAT!... IT WILL SAVE WEAR AND TEAR ON YOUR ACTING ABILITY!
ASIDE FROM THE FACT THAT I READ THE CODE REPORT OF YOUR SECRET POLICE COLLEAGUES ON HOW YOU WERE DOING TRYING TO INCRIMINATE ME WITH MY GOVERNMENT....
...I KNEW YOUR PURPOSE FROM THE MOMENT YOU SAID YOU WERE MRS. KAMP, WIFE OF ONE OF THE SECRET POLICEMEN OUT HERE! WHEN KAMP LEFT THIS HOUSE ON HIS WAY TO THE INTERIOR, HE GAVE ME A LETTER...TO BE SENT TO HIS WIFE IN PARIS — WHOM HE MARRIED SECRETLY, BECAUSE SHE WAS FRENCH — IN CASE HE FAILED TO RETURN!
MILTON CANIFF

OKAY, WOLFF! IT'S YOUR BALL!...YOU'RE RIGHT...I WAS SENT HERE BY THE SECRET POLICE OF YOUR GOVERNMENT...WHAT ARE YOU GOING TO DO ABOUT IT?
DO ABOUT IT?...NOTHING AT ALL! I KNOW WHY THEY WISH TO HAVE EVIDENCE AGAINST ME...
6-6
Reg. U. S. Pat. Off.: Copyright, 1941, by News Syndicate Co. Inc.
MY GOVERNMENT'S METHODS ARE ANOTHER MATTER!... I'M WONDERING ABOUT YOU! WHY SHOULD AN AMERICAN BE PART OF A SYSTEM IN WHICH UNITY MAY BE MAINTAINED ONLY BY EVERY PERSON BEING SUSPICIOUS OF EVERY OTHER PERSON?
DO YOU KNOW WHAT MILLIONS OF PEOPLE WOULD GIVE TO BE A CITIZEN OF ONE OF THE FEW NATIONS ON EARTH WHERE THE INDIVIDUAL STILL HAS THE DIGNITY OF FREEDOM?
BUT...
...THERE ARE NO BUTS!...YOU PEOPLE CAN WALK OUT OF YOUR HOUSES EVERY DAY...GO WHERE YOU LIKE, SAY WHAT YOU LIKE, WORSHIP AS YOU LIKE...AND WAVE TO THE POLICEMAN ON THE CORNER, INSTEAD OF SHOWING HIM YOUR PAPERS!! ...AND WHY DO I KNOW THIS?...BECAUSE ONLY PEOPLE IN PRISON KNOW HOW IT ONCE FELT TO BE FREE!....
MILTON CANIFF

I THOUGHT YOU'D SOCK ME, INSTEAD OF LECTURING ME, WHEN YOU LEARNED I CAME HERE TO GET EVIDENCE AGAINST YOU FOR YOUR COUNTRY'S SECRET POLICE!
IF IT HADN'T BEEN YOU IT WOULD HAVE BEEN SOME OTHER PARTY SPY!...I'M TALKING TO YOU BECAUSE YOU'RE AN AMERICAN!
6-7
Reg. U. S. Pat. Off.: Copyright, 1941, by News Syndicate Co. Inc.
IT ISN'T WHAT GOVERNMENTS FIGHT OVER...TRADE, POWER AND SO ON... IT'S WHAT HAPPENS TO PEOPLE WHEN THOSE FIGHTS OCCUR! YOU CITIZENS OF DEMOCRACIES HAVE MORE INDIVIDUAL FREEDOM THAN ANY PEOPLE ON EARTH... AND MOST OF YOU DON'T EVEN KNOW IT!
...I DON'T KNOW WHY YOU'RE IN THIS SPY BUSINESS — BUT IF I WERE YOU, I'D GO TO BED...AND THANK WHATEVER DEITY YOU HAVE THE FREEDOM OF WORSHIPPING — THAT YOU ARE NOT A SLAVE TO ANYONE!
HA! WE WERE WISE TO CUT THIS HOLE THROUGH THE WALL BEHIND THE SCREEN IN WOLFF'S LIVING ROOM!
...SO! WE HAVE ENOUGH EVIDENCE TO SATISFY OUR SUPERIOR! THE WOMAN DID WELL!
MILTON CANIFF

Reg. U. S. Pat. Off.:
Copyright, 1941, by News Syndicate Co., Inc.
TERRY AND THE PIRATES
by MILTON CANIFF
WHAT'S THIS?... COLONEL WOLFF WILL BE RELIEVED OF HIS POST AT THE DAM... HE WILL BE CONFINED TO QUARTERS UNDER ARREST, PENDING FURTHER ORDERS! NEXT IN COMMAND WILL TAKE OVER...."
...AND SIGNED BY THE TIN SOLDIER IN COMMAND OF THIS AREA! ...THAT PUTS YOU IN THE SADDLE, SHERLOCK! WHAT IS THE CHARGE?
TREASONABLE UTTERANCES AGAINST THE HIGH COMMAND! ...YOU DID WELL, MISS!
YOU MEAN THE CONVERSATION MR. WOLFF AND I HAD BEFORE THE FIRE...? BUT I REPEATED NOTHING...
YOU DIDN'T NEED TO! —YOUR LITTLE FRIENDS CUT A LISTENING HOLE THROUGH THE WALL BEHIND THIS SILK PANEL! I FOUND IT THIS MORNING! YOU MAY GO BACK TO YOUR SUPERIORS AND TELL THEM HOW CLEVER YOU ARE!
HERE ARE MY KEYS AND BOOKS! I FLATTER MYSELF THAT I GOT WORK OUT OF THAT POLYGLOT SHOVEL GANG ON THE DAM BY TREATING THE MEN LIKE HUMAN BEINGS ... I WARN YOU NOT TO TRY OTHER METHODS! I WILL BE IN MY ROOM... IF YOU NEED ME!
—BUT WHEN THE TWO SECRET POLICEMEN TAKE OVER WOLFF'S DUTIES......
...IT WILL BE MUCH TO OUR CREDIT IF WE FINISH THIS DAM WHILE WOLFF AWAITS TRIAL!
WE THINK ALIKE! I WILL DOUBLE THE SHIFTS — AFTER ALL, THIS IS SLAVE LABOR SUCH AS THE LEADER DESCRIBES!
AS THE WORKING DAY GOES INTO THREE EIGHT-HOUR SHIFTS, TERRY NOTICES WORD BEING PASSED AMONG THE CHINESE....
WOLFF WAS CLEVER... THESE NEW ENGINEERS ARE FOOLS! THEY DO THE ONE THING WE HAVE WAITED FOR! SEND A COURIER TO THE TELEGRAPH LINE! THE TIME IS NOW!
WISH I KNEW WHAT THOSE GUERILLAS ARE COOKIN' UP! THE TWO SECRET COPS KEEP BURMA GUARDED — BUT IF SOMETHING BREAKS WE MIGHT BE ABLE TO GET AWAY! THERE'S THE GONG FOR THE SHIFTS TO CHANGE! GOTTA LEAVE THE LANTERNS FOR THE NEW MEN... GOLLY, BUT I'M TIRED!
THE NEW CREW MUST WAIT UNTIL THE RETIRING GANG CLEARS THE NARROW CAT-WALKS OF THE DAM STRUCTURE....
THOSE CHINESE ARE SINGING TONIGHT FOR SOME REASON! MUST BE ONE OF THEIR SILLY RELIGIOUS CUSTOMS! WHAT A DIN!
...AT THE PRECISE MOMENT WHEN THE HUGE PROJECT IS CLEAR OF MEN.....
...STOP CROWDING HERE WITH YOUR CRAZY YELPING!... LOOK! A ROCKET!
AND LISTEN! I CAN HEAR ANOTHER SOUND ABOVE THE SQUAWKING!... PLANES!
DOWN TO THE EMPTY DAM, PERFECTLY OUTLINED BY THE WORKMEN'S LANTERNS, ROARS A SQUADRON OF CHINESE BOMBERS...
6-8

6-9
Reg. U. S. Pat. Off., Copyright, 1941, by News Syndicate Co. Inc.
CHINESE PLANES BOMBING THE DAM!!.. GUERILLAS MUST HAVE TIPPED 'EM OFF WHEN THOSE TWO SECRET POLICE STOOGES TOOK OVER WOLFF'S POSITION AND PUT US ON A NIGHT SHIFT....
THE PLANES WOULDN'T HAVE RISKED DAY BOMBING... THE LIGHTS ON THE DAM MUST HAVE GUIDED THEM AT NIGHT! WOW!....THE CHINESE ARE ATTACKING THE GUARDS!...
MUST GET TO BURMA...
THAT ONE IS IN LEAGUE WITH THE INVADER! I SAW HIM GO BY NIGHT TO HOUSE OF WOLFF!
MILTON CANIFF

HOLY CATS! THE CHINESE HAVE GONE DAFFY SINCE THE DAM WAS BOMBED! THEY MUST THINK I'M CONNECTED WITH THE BOSSES IN SOME WAY!
6-10
Reg. U. S. Pat. Off., Copyright, 1941, by News Syndicate Co. Inc.
THERE GO THE TWO SECRET POLICEMEN WHO BROUGHT BURMA HERE!... THEY HAVE GUNS!... I'LL HAVE TO JOIN UP WITH THEM —OR BE MOBBED!
HEY! I'M AN AMERICAN! ...IF WE COLLECT SOME OF THE GUARDS WE CAN MAKE A STAND! THEY'RE AFTER ME, TOO!
MILTON CANIFF

THAT BOY FOLLOWING US... HE SPOKE IN ENGLISH!
LET HIM LOOK OUT FOR HIMSELF!... TELEPHONE THE ARMY AIRPORT FOR THE PARACHUTE TROOPS ...WHILE I HOLD OFF THIS RABBLE!
6-11
Reg. U. S. Pat. Off., Copyright, 1941, by News Syndicate Co. Inc.
THE ...BOMBS ...HAVE...CUT ...THE...LINE!
...CAN'T STAND THERE POUNDIN' ON A DOOR! THAT MOB'S BOILIN'! MAYBE THEY'LL FORGET ME UP HERE—WITH THOSE GUYS INSIDE BLAZING AWAY!
YOW! THEY'RE GOING TO BURN US OUT!
MILTON CANIFF

THAT MOB OF CONSTRUCTION WORKERS IS TRYING TO SMOKE OUT THE TWO SECRET COPS DOWNSTAIRS...AND ME TOO!... GOLLY—AND I DON'T EVEN KNOW WHAT'S HAPPENED TO BURMA!
6-12
Reg. U. S. Pat. Off., Copyright, 1941, by News Syndicate Co. Inc.
FIRE'S...COMING...CLOSER! SMOKE'S...SO...THICK ...CAN'T SEE...
MILTON CANIFF

6-13
Reg. U. S. Pat. Off.; Copyright, 1941, by News Syndicate Co. Inc.
GOOD OLD GOOEY DIRT! FROM NOW ON THE WORD 'DUMPY' IS A COMPLIMENT!... GOTTA GET TO WOLFF'S HOUSE AND FIND BURMA!
MILTON CANIFF
YOOPS!
6-14
Reg. U. S. Pat. Off.; Copyright, 1941, by News Syndicate Co. Inc.
MUST BE SOME OF THE GUERILLA LEADERS LOOKING FOR WOLFF! — BUT HE ISN'T WITH THEM!... MAYBE THEY FOUND HIM AND BURMA AND--- WHAT'S THAT?
DON'T BE ALARMED, BOY! THESE BOMB SHELTERS SOMETIMES HAVE OTHER USES!
MILTON CANIFF
Reg. U. S. Pat. Off.; Copyright, 1941, by News Syndicate Co. Inc.
TERRY AND THE PIRATES
by MILTON CANIFF
THE CONSTRUCTION CREW HAS TURNED INTO A HOWLING MOB! THE MEN WHO ARRANGED THE BOMBING HAVE LOST CONTROL!
THEY WILL BE AFTER ME — AS A SYMBOL OF THE INVADER ACTIVITY! WHAT'S WORSE — THEY'LL TREAT YOU AS A FRIEND OF MINE!
WHY DO YOU TRY TO PROTECT US — WHEN I CAME HERE TO HELP INJURE YOU, WOLFF?
NO TIME TO GO INTO THAT!... MY CAR IS STILL INTACT... WE JUST MIGHT BE ABLE TO GET AWAY TO OPEN COUNTRY!
GOOD THING I BLACKED MY HAIR — OR THEY WOULD HAVE SHOT ME AS ONE OF YOUR BOYS!... LISTEN! THE GANG'S ON IT'S WAY HERE NOW!
YOU TWO GO OUT TO THE AUTOMOBILE — AND WARM THE MOTOR!... I MUST BRING ONE IMPORTANT THING FROM MY ROOM!
OKE!
... HERE HE COMES, TERRY! ... AND I STILL DON'T SEE WHY HE WANTS TO HELP US!
... LOOK IN ANY MIRROR FOR THE ANSWER TO THAT, BURMA!.... YOW! HERE COMES THE MOB, TOO!

MUCH LATER...

MUSTA SLEPT! ...BURMA, WHERE'S MR. WOLFF?
OH... I-- LOOK!
YOUR SURPRISE IS UNDERSTANDABLE! WE WILL CONTINUE THE JOURNEY UNDER SOMEWHAT DIFFERENT CIRCUMSTANCES!
6-15

MUSTA BEEN ASLEEP... GEE, BURMA, IT WAS NICE OF MR. WOLFF TO GET US AWAY FROM THE BOMBING IN HIS CAR... WE SHOULD BE SAFE ENOUGH BY NOW!
TERRY! LOOK!
6-16
Reg. U. S. Pat. Off.
Copyright, 1941, by News Syndicate Co. Inc.
THE BOY SEEMS PUZZLED! DID HE NOT KNOW THAT I AM A COLONEL OF ENGINEERS IN MY COUNTRY'S ARMY?
I GUESSED THAT... BUT WHY DID YOU STOP AND PUT ON THE UNIFORM, MR. WOLFF?
THE CHINESE WHO CARRIED OUT THE BOMBING OF THE DAM WILL CUT THE RAIL LINE!... THE AUTOMOBILE IS OUR ONLY MEANS OF REACHING A CITY!
I WEAR THE UNIFORM BECAUSE IT IMPRESSES THE SOLDIERS OCCUPYING THIS PART OF CHINA! THE SECRET POLICE WILL WANT THEIR BLONDE SIREN RETURNED SAFELY.... SO SHE MAY BE SENT TO HELP INCRIMINATE SOME OTHER OFFICER WHO IS LUKE-WARM ON POLITICS!
MILTON CANIFF

SO YOU WEAR YOUR UNIFORM TO IMPRESS THE INVADER SOLDIERS IN OCCUPIED CHINA? WHAT DOES THAT MAKE US, COLONEL WOLFF?
I MUST CONTACT THE NEAREST ARMY OUTPOST TO REPORT THE BOMBING AND GET A COUNTER-ATTACK UNDER WAY!...
6-17
Copyright, 1941, by News Syndicate Co. Inc.
TO AVOID COMPLICATIONS, YOU WILL DRIVE THE CAR... AS IF YOU ARE ONE OF MY MEN... THE YOUNG LADY AND I WILL RIDE TOGETHER!
OKAY... YOU'RE MR. BIG AROUND HERE... BUT WHAT HAPPENS TO US THEN?... DO WE GO ON PLAYING STOOGE TO YOU?
MILTON CANIFF
...YOU MAY RECALL THAT YOU ESCAPED FROM A PRISON CAMP NOT LONG AGO! I RECEIVED A DESCRIPTION OF YOU—SINCE ESCAPED PRISONERS OFTEN TRY TO GET WORK ON CONSTRUCTION PROJECTS!... YOU MENTIONED BEFORE THAT YOU HAD BLACKED YOUR HAIR! WHEN I TURN YOU IN IT WILL OFFSET THE EVIDENCE THIS WOMAN HAS AGAINST ME!

SO YOU'RE GOING TO TURN ME IN AS AN ESCAPED PRISONER— TO OFFSET THE EVIDENCE AGAINST YOU THAT BURMA CAN GIVE THE SECRET POLICE!
PRECISELY! IF YOU ARE THINKING OF TRYING TO ESCAPE, REMEMBER THAT I HAVE A VERY EFFICIENT PISTOL IN MY HAND!
6-18
Reg. U. S. Pat. Off.; Copyright, 1941, by News Syndicate Co. Inc.
I COULD DUMP HIS CAR IN A DITCH AND FIX US ALL...
YOU ARE NOT SUCH A FOOL! BE QUIET!
WE ARE APPROACHING AN ARMY OUTPOST! I WILL MAKE MY REPORT HERE...AND PERHAPS TURN YOU OVER TO THE GUARDS TO BE SENT BACK TO PRISON!
AND WHAT DO YOU PROPOSE TO DO ABOUT ME?
I HAVEN'T DECIDED! ..SINCE THOSE TWO SECRET POLICEMEN ARE PROBABLY DEAD, YOU ARE THE ONLY PERSON WHO COULD TESTIFY AGAINST ME AT A COURT-MARTIAL! IT WOULD BE PLEASANT IF YOU FAILED TO RETURN!
MILTON CANIFF

YOU WILL LEAVE THE CAR AND WALK AHEAD OF ME INTO THE BUILDING... WHERE I WILL MAKE MY REPORT OF THE BOMBING OF THE DAM!
6-19
Reg. U. S. Pat. Off.; Copyright, 1941, by News Syndicate Co. Inc.
SO YOUR FRIEND WOLFF IS 'NOT A BAD EGG'... OH, GOLLY, BURMA, I THOUGHT YOU WERE A BETTER JUDGE OF PEOPLE!
I MUST ADMIT... IT DOESN'T ADD UP!... HE'S HAD US LOCKED IN HERE FOR AN HOUR!
WHEN HE GETS A COUNTER-ATTACK GOING AGAINST THE GUERILLAS AT THE DAM HE CAN DO ANYTHING HE LIKES WITH US... NO CHANCE OF ESCAPE IN THIS OCCUPIED AREA!
WE WILL HAVE QUITE A WAIT UNTIL THE TROOPS MOVE UP TO RE-TAKE THE DAM!... NO REASON WHY THE INTERVAL SHOULDN'T BE PLEASANT! COME WITH ME, WOMAN!
MILTON CANIFF

BURMA! DON'T---
QUIET, BOY! SHE'S GOING WITH ME— BECAUSE SHE HAS NO CHOICE!
6-20
Reg. U. S. Pat. Off.; Copyright, 1941, by News Syndicate Co. Inc.
WELL, HOW DO YOU LIKE IT?
LIKE WHAT? DO I HAVE TO ANSWER RIDDLES, TOO?
I MEAN, HOW DO YOU LIKE THE DEMONSTRATION OF WHAT IT IS LIKE TO LIVE UNDER A SYSTEM WHERE A PERSON WITH A FANCY UNIFORM AND A TITLE CAN BOOT YOUR PRIVATE LIFE AROUND?
MILTON CANIFF
WHAT IS THIS, A GAG? DID YOU DRAG ME OUT HERE TO READ ME A LECTURE?
YES, IN A WAY! I HAVE TRIED TO GIVE YOU AND THE BOY A DEMONSTRATION, IN REVERSE, OF HOW FORTUNATE YOU ARE TO BE AMERICANS!

YOU MEAN YOU'VE BEEN KICKING TERRY AND ME AROUND TO SHOW US WHAT IT'S LIKE TO LIVE UNDER THE HEEL OF A HEEL?
RIGHT! WHERE A PERSON MAY BE A FRIEND ONE MINUTE— AND AN ENEMY THE NEXT—IF HE'S AFRAID YOU HAVE SOMETHING ON HIM!
6-21
Reg. U. S. Pat. Off.; Copyright, 1941, by News Syndicate Co. Inc.
MANY OF US IN MY COUNTRY ENVY YOUR FREEDOM... BUT WE'RE AFRAID TO MENTION IT TO OUR CLOSEST FRIENDS! IF YOU AMERICANS KNEW WHAT IT WAS LIKE TO HAVE YOUR MINDS IMPRISONED IN YOUR OWN BODIES, YOU WOULD BE MORE JEALOUS OF YOUR LIBERTY!
A VERY PRETTY SPEECH, MY FINE-FEATHERED FRIEND —BUT THE FACT REMAINS THAT TERRY AND I ARE YOUR PRISONERS... DEEP IN OCCUPIED TERRITORY!
THAT'S WHY I HAVE TRIED TO SHOW YOU WHAT TYRANNY IS LIKE... BECAUSE I AM GOING TO SEE THAT YOU GET AWAY INTO FREE CHINA —AND I WANT YOU TO KNOW HOW SWEET FREE AIR CAN TASTE!
MILTON CANIFF

TERRY
MILTON CANIFF
THIS COUNTRY HAS BEEN FOUGHT OVER RECENTLY! WE WILL STOP AND CHECK OUR DIRECTIONS!
REMEMBER! WE ARE IN OCCUPIED TERRITORY — AND YOU TWO ARE IN MY CUSTODY! DO NOT MOVE FROM THE CAR!...
OH, SURE! YOU'RE 'PROTECTING' US, AREN'T YOU, COLONEL WOLFF?
WELL, BURMA, WE'RE WORSE OFF THAN EVER! YOU SAID THIS WOLFF WAS A GOOD EGG — BUT WHAT A BULLY-BOY HE TURNS OUT TO BE WITH THAT UNIFORM ON!
YOU SAID HE PUT OUT A LOT OF TALK ABOUT HOW HE LOVES FREEDOM TO WORK AS HE PLEASES — BUT THAT HE IS A SOLDIER OF HIS COUNTRY.... WHERE THE HABIT OF OBEDIENCE IS GROUND INTO EVERY YOUNG MAN....
...HE SAID HE ENVIED US BEING AMERICANS — THEN HE GETS DOGGED UP IN HIS FANCY DUDS AND TREATS US AS HIS PRISONERS — EVEN THOUGH HE KNOWS YOU WERE SENT TO GET HIM IN TROUBLE! IT DOESN'T MAKE SENSE!... HERE HE COMES NOW — WITH AN INVADER BRASS HAT!
THE CHINESE GUERILLAS HAVE CUT THE ROAD BETWEEN US AND THE CITY! THERE WAS A BATTLE HERE ONLY YESTERDAY... THE CHINESE LINES ARE JUST OVER THE HILL...
RAISE YOUR HANDS! ...GET UNDER THE WHEEL AND STEP ON IT, TERRY!
GET A CAR TO CAPTURE THEM, YOU FOOL!
BUT IT WOULD BE SUICIDE, MASTER... THEY GO STRAIGHT TOWARD THE ENEMY LINES!
NICE GOIN', BURMA!... THEY'RE SHOOTING TOO HIGH TO HIT US!
...BEHOLD! A FIRE CART APPROACHES! I CAN DESTROY IT WITH A BURST!...
IT IS NOT AN ATTACK! ALLOW THE THING TO PASS! IF IT IS A TRICK WE CAN SMASH THE OCCUPANTS WELL INSIDE OUR LINES!
...YIPPEE! WE MADE IT! I'LL PULL UP — SO THE GUERILLAS WILL KNOW WE'RE NOT INVADERS! ...YOU SURE CROSSED OLD WOLFF UP! HOW DID YOU GET THE GUN?
6-22
WOLFF SAW THAT WE TOOK THE ROAD THAT WOULD COME NEAREST THE FRONT... HE GAVE ME THE GUN LAST NIGHT AND TOLD ME TO PULL THE ESCAPE IN FRONT OF A WITNESS, WHEN THE STAGE WAS SET!... HE SHOT OVER OUR HEADS TO MAKE IT LOOK REAL!... FUNNY WORLD, ISN'T IT?

BEHOLD, CAPTAIN, A LONE FIRE CART DASHED FROM THE INVADER LINES! IS IT NOT AN ODD OCCURRENCE?
EVEN MORE SO IS THE PRESENCE OF A WOMAN WITH YELLOW HAIR!
6-23
Reg. U. S. Pat. Off.; Copyright, 1941, by News Syndicate Co. Inc.
EASY, TERRY! WE DON'T WANT THE CHINESE TO BLOW OUR TOPS — AFTER SHAKING THE INVADERS SO SMOOTHLY!
I'M IN A DAZE! JUST WHEN I THOUGHT THAT WOLFF GUY WAS A NUMBER ONE LOUSE...
...HE SLIPS YOU A GUN — SO WE CAN STAGE A GET-AWAY IN FRONT OF WITNESSES! HOW DO YOU FIGURE IT?
HE SAID HE WANTED US TO KNOW HOW TYRANNY FELT — SO WE COULD REALLY APPRECIATE FREEDOM WHEN WE GOT IT!
UP THE HANDS! YOU NOW PRISONERS!
MILTON CANIFF
MAYBE WE'RE OUT OF THE PAN AND INTO THE HEAT, BURMA!
IT'S BETTER THAN HAVING AN AXIS TO GRIND, TERRY!
COME! MAKE TALK WITH HIGH OFFICER!
6-24
Reg. U. S. Pat. Off.; Copyright, 1941, by News Syndicate Co. Inc.
THEY THINK WE'RE SPIES!
NATURALLY! DON'T TELL THEM ABOUT WOLFF HELPING US! SAY WE SWIPED THE CAR!
THEY DIDN'T SEARCH US! I'D BETTER GIVE THEM WOLFF'S GUN BEFORE THEY FIND IT... HEY! WHAT TH--
MILTON CANIFF
NO, NO! YOU GUYS HAVE SEEN TOO MANY MOVIES! I'M GIVING YOU THE GUN....SINCE YOU NEGLECTED TO SEARCH US!
6-25
Reg. U. S. Pat. Off.; Copyright, 1941, by News Syndicate Co. Inc.
THE SOLDIER THINKS HE'S LOST FACE! NOW HE SEEMS TO BE PLEADING FOR US! THIS IS THE TIME TO TELL OUR STORY!
...AND THAT'S THE WAY IT WAS! WE JUST GRABBED THE AUTOMOBILE AND RACED FOR YOUR LINES!...
AND WHAT DOES MY CAPTAIN MAKE OF THIS GREAT TALE TOLD BY THE YOUNG ONE?
THEY SEEM TO TRY TO BE FRIENDLY!...BUT THE ENEMY KNOWS MANY TRICKS! BID THEM WELCOME HERE...THEN WATCH EVERY MOVE! IF THEY ARE SPIES, THEY WILL EXPOSE THE FACT IN SOME MANNER!
MILTON CANIFF
COMMANDING ONE SAY YOU STAY THIS PLACE! VILLAGE FULL OF REFUGEES!
BETTER THAN NO SHELTER AT ALL! THANKS, SOLDIER!
6-26
Reg. U. S. Pat. Off.; Copyright, 1941, by News Syndicate Co. Inc.
LATER
IS IT POSSIBLE TO OBSERVE THE MOVEMENTS OF THE STRANGERS FROM THIS POINT?
EVEN SO, MY CAPTAIN... BUT SUSPICIOUS EVENTS TAKE PLACE!
THE MALE ONE REQUESTED SHOVELS AND BUCKETS! THEN BUILT A FIRE... BUT HE HAS HEATED ENOUGH WATER TO MAKE TEA FOR THE ENTIRE ARMY! IT IS HIGHLY IRREGULAR!
THAT'S ENOUGH, TERRY! LET THE INVADERS BOMB THE PLACE! BURMA HAS FOUND PEACE!
MILTON CANIFF

BURMA'S A NEW WOMAN! IT'S YOUR TURN, TERRY! AND FOR PETE'S SAKE, WASH THAT BLACK STUFF OUT OF YOUR HAIR!
GEE! DO YOU REALLY CARE HOW I LOOK, BURMA?
6-27
Reg. U. S. Pat. Off.: Copyright, 1941, by News Syndicate Co. Inc.
SURE! IF I HAVE TO CARRY BATH WATER FOR A GUY, I WANT IT TO DO SOME GOOD!
LATER
KINDA TOUGH WITHOUT SOAP ... BUT NOW WE LOOK LIKE A BROTHER AND SISTER ACT AGAIN!
OKAY, BRUDDER! SEE IF YOU CAN DIG UP SOME GRUB FOR THE FAMILY!
COME QUICKLY, MY CAPTAIN! THE STRANGERS ARE SPIES! THE INCRIMINATING EVIDENCE IS AT HAND!
MILTON CANIFF

WHAT'S THIS? WHY THE ARTILLERY?
YOU WERE OBSERVED AS YOU CHANGED IDENTITIES!
BUT HE SIMPLY WASHED HIS HAIR!
6-28
Reg. U. S. Pat. Off.: Copyright, 1941, by News Syndicate Co. Inc.
SO! WHY WAS THE HAIR BLACK?
WELL—IT WAS A SORT OF DISGUISE!
AH-HA!
BUT YOU CAN'T DO THIS TO US!
MILTON CANIFF

Reg. U. S. Pat. Off.: Copyright, 1941, by News Syndicate Co. Inc.
TERRY AND THE PIRATES
by MILTON CANIFF
AFTER WOLFF RISKED HIS NECK TO GET US INTO FREE CHINA — THE GUERILLAS TOSS US IN THE JUG AS SPIES! FINE THING, SAYS BURMA!
THIS BUNCH IS REALLY A RAIDING PARTY!... THE COMMANDER IS AFRAID OF BEING ENCIRCLED AND CUT OFF FROM HIS BASE! THE WAY WE CAME HERE WOULD MAKE ANYONE SUSPICIOUS!
SURE, TERRY, I KNOW... BUT THAT DOESN'T KEEP MY FEET WARM!
I MENTIONED ALL THE PEOPLE I KNOW IN THE CHINESE FORCES... HE SAID HE'D CHECK ON US BY TELEGRAPH! WE SHOULD BE OUT IN NO TIME! ...I HOPE!!...
GEE, I WONDER WHO'S WEARING ALL THOSE CLOTHES I LEFT BEHIND! I CAN'T LAY UP AN EXTRA CHEMISE FOR A HARD WINTER! I KNOW WHO'S LOSING THIS WAR... IT'S BURMA!
THESE CHINESE TROOPS ARE PROBABLY WAITING IN THE TOWN UNTIL DARK TO MAKE A RUN FOR IT! THIS IS DANGEROUS COUNTRY! ...HEY! LISTEN!... PLANES!
THERE GOES A BOMB... THAT WAS AT THE EDGE OF TOWN!... THE INVADERS MUST HAVE HEARD THE TROOPS WERE HERE!
WOW! BOMBS AND MACHINE GUNS! LOOK AT THOSE WOMEN AND KIDS MILLING ABOUT! THEY ACT AS IF THEY'VE NEVER BEEN RAIDED BEFORE!
TERRY! WE'RE IN THE ONLY DECENT SHELTER IN TOWN! ...AND THE GUARD'S BEEN HIT! WE'VE GOT TO GET THOSE SPROUTS IN HERE!

LATER.... WHEN THE BOMBERS HAVE ROARED AWAY....
6-29

MY SUPERIOR APPEARS MOST AGITATED!
AND WHO WOULD NOT BE? ANSWER ME THAT! SHUT UP!... DON'T TALK BACK!... A BAND OF THE ACCURSED GUERILLAS MOVES INTO MY TERRITORY ... JUST AS MY FLOWER GARDEN WAS BECOMING INTERESTING!
THE HIGH COMMAND ORDERS THEM REMOVED ... BY POSTING 'NO ADMITTANCE' SIGNS, I PRESUME!
I SEND TROOPS... THE GUERILLAS HIDE THEIR GUNS AND UNIFORMS AND BECOME FARMERS! I CANNOT SHOOT THE FARMERS BECAUSE THEY RAISE THE FOOD FOR MY TROOPS! THIS IS NOT WAR... IT IS A MASQUERADE!
...BUT WE DO KNOW THE VILLAGE THEY USE AS HEADQUARTERS... PERHAPS WE CAN EMPLOY THE METHODS OF OUR ALLIES IN EUROPE! THE SEED OF PANIC GROWS INTO A USEFUL WEED!
MILTON CANIFF
6-30

SIRE! I HAVE BROUGHT TWO MEN TRAINED IN THE LOCAL DIALECT! THEY READILY PASS AS CHINESE!
GOOD! NOW GIVE EAR TO MY PLAN FOR DISLODGING THESE GUERILLAS!
IN THE HEADQUARTERS OF THE GUERILLA TROOPS...
THESE SOLDIERS DON'T KNOW WHAT TO MAKE OF US, BURMA! THEY THOUGHT WE WERE SPIES, UNTIL WE HELPED THE CIVILIANS DURING AN AIR RAID!
BUT THEY'RE STILL NOT GIVING US PASSES FOR SIGHTSEEING TOURS! THIS PLACE IS TOO NEAR THE INVADER LINES FOR COMFORT!
ON THE OUTSKIRTS OF THE GUERILLA VILLAGE...
BEHOLD OUR PLIGHT AND TAKE WARNING! THE INVADER COMES TO BURN YOUR HOUSE AND KILL YOUR FAMILY! REFUGEE TO THE WEST BEFORE IT IS TOO LATE!
THE INVADER WILL SLAUGHTER US FOR HIDING GUERILLA TROOPS!... REFUGEE WEST!
MILTON CANIFF
7-1

OTHER CANIFF BOOKS FROM NBM:

TERRY & THE PIRATES COLLECTOR'S EDITION SPECIAL SALE!
Beautiful hardbound volumes, gold stamped, 320 pp. each, jacketed. Normally $36.50 each; NOW ONLY $19.95!

Volumes remaining: 7 (1940-'41), 8 ('41-'42), 10 ('43-'44), 11 ('44-'45), 12 ('45-'46).

"MILTON CANIFF, REMBRANDT OF THE COMIC STRIP"
Biography of Caniff with an introduction by comics historian Rick Marschall, editor of Nemo. Many rare illustrations and stunning blow-ups of Caniff's art.
Paperback, 64 pp., 8½x11: $6.95

GET 'EM HOT OFF THE PRESS! SUBSCRIBE!
This Terry & the Pirates reprint is quarterly like clockwork. Make sure to get each new volume hot off the press, sent in a sturdy carton mailer. You can start with any volume, past or future!
$25 for 4 volumes

MISSING ANY PAST VOLUMES?
Vol. 1 Welcome to China (1934) $6.95
Vol. 2 Marooned with Burma (1935) $5.95
Vol. 3 Dragon Lady's Revenge (1936) $5.95
Vol. 4 Getting Snared (1936-37) $5.95
Vol. 5 Shanghaied (1937) $5.95
Vol. 6 The Warlord Klang (1937-38) $6.95
Vol. 7 The Hunter (1938) $6.95
Vol. 8 The Baron (1938-39) $6.95
Vol. 9 Feminine Venom (1939) $6.95
Vol. 10 Network of Intrigue (1939-40) $6.95
Vol. 11 Gal Got Our Pal (1940) $6.95
Vol. 12 Flying Ace Dude (1940-41) $6.95

HANDSOME SLIPCASED SETS
4 volumes in each for a total of 256 pages of intense reading, slipcased in a leathery cloth, gold-stamped with the Terry logo.
Vols. 1-4: $29.50
Vols. 5-8: $29.50
Vols. 9-12: $29.50
SLIPCASE ALONE: $7.50

P&H: Add $2 first item, $1 each addt'l. No P&H on subscriptions!

NBM
35-53 70th St.
Jackson Heights, NY 11372

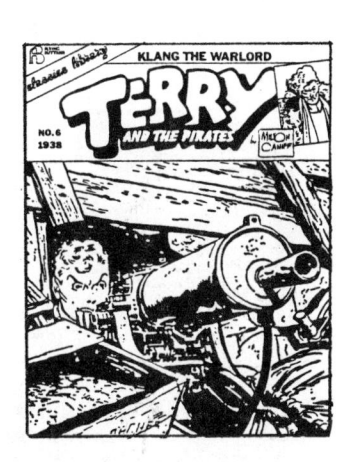

Flying Buttress Classics Library

announces:

the complete

WASH TUBBS & CAPTAIN EASY

by ROY CRANE

1924 – 1943

The Flying Buttress Classics Library, announces a new reprint: Roy Crane's classic WASH TUBBS (1924-1943). Wash Tubbs was Crane's first strip, and already with it he set the pace for future adventure strips to match, including Terry & The Pirates. Wash Tubbs exemplifies two-fisted adventure spiced with a good sense of humor. Wash and his pals, Gozzy Gallup and **Captain Easy**, battle arch villians Bull Dawson and Shanghai Slug in exotic locales on land and sea around the world.

Each volume of this quarterly **18 volume complete reprint** will contain 192 pages of action. Like our recently completed Terry & The Pirates series, you can count on high quality and regular publishing schedules. Both hardcover and paperback will be available in a large but handy 11 by 8 1/2 format. Each volume will print approximately one year's worth of strips. Sundays are included.

PAPERBACK EDITION:
$16.95 each
(add $2.00 postage & handling)

HARDCOVER EDITION
$32.50 each
(add $2.00 postage & handling)

Vols. 1-8 available

SEVEN CENTURIES AGO GHENGIS KHAN AND HIS HORDE OF SAVAGE MONGOLS OVER-RAN ALL CHINA.

SPECIAL OFFER:
Order your subscription to any 4 hardcover volumes and pay only $80!
Also available: you can subscribe to the paperback edition for $50 for **any** four. (no p + h for subs)

NBM
35-53 70th St.
Jackson Heights, NY 11372